Frontier Manicure

Longarm's left fist shot out like the head of a snake and his knuckles smashed into the man's nose, breaking it and sending him reeling backward. When the other two jumped forward, Longarm's right hand crossed his belt buckle and snapped his Colt from its holster on his left hip. The gun came up and the two men dropped their knives in the dirt and fled.

The man Longarm had smashed in the nose was cupping it with both hands, blood dripping between his fingers.

"Damn you!" the injured man cried. "We only wanted a couple of lousy dollars!"

"Tell you what," Longarm said, "I'll give you something that will last longer than a few dollars."

"What . . ."

Longarm smashed the barrel of his heavy Colt across the man's forehead, knocking him out cold.

"Custis!" Milly said, hurrying to catch up with him. "That man will need stitches in his scalp and his nose is really a mess!"

"You think I was too rough on him, do you? Milly, I told you you wouldn't be prepared for what faced us up here. We haven't even come face to face with the worst of it yet and already you're starting to tell me what to do and what not to do."

"I don't mean to do that, Custis, but you really hurt that man!"

"And what do you think they intended to do with those knives they pulled? Clip our fingernails?"

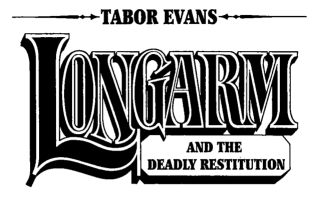

TABOR EVANS

LONGARM

AND THE
DEADLY RESTITUTION

JOVE BOOKS, NEW YORK

THE BERKLEY PUBLISHING GROUP
Published by the Penguin Group
Penguin Group (USA) Inc.
375 Hudson Street, New York, New York 10014, USA
Penguin Group (Canada), 90 Eglinton Avenue East, Suite 700, Toronto, Ontario M4P 2Y3, Canada
(a division of Pearson Penguin Canada Inc.) • Penguin Books Ltd., 80 Strand, London WC2R 0RL,
England • Penguin Group Ireland, 25 St. Stephen's Green, Dublin 2, Ireland (a division of Penguin
Books Ltd.) • Penguin Group (Australia), 250 Camberwell Road, Camberwell, Victoria 3124, Australia
(a division of Pearson Australia Group Pty. Ltd.) • Penguin Books India Pvt. Ltd., 11 Community
Centre, Panchsheel Park, New Delhi—110 017, India • Penguin Group (NZ), 67 Apollo Drive,
Rosedale, Auckland 0632, New Zealand (a division of Pearson New Zealand Ltd.) • Penguin Books
(South Africa) (Pty.) Ltd., 24 Sturdee Avenue, Rosebank, Johannesburg 2196, South Africa

Penguin Books Ltd., Registered Offices: 80 Strand, London WC2R 0RL, England

This is a work of fiction. Names, characters, places, and incidents either are the product of the author's imagination or are used fictitiously, and any resemblance to actual persons, living or dead, business establishments, events, or locales is entirely coincidental.

LONGARM AND THE DEADLY RESTITUTION

A Jove Book / published by arrangement with the author

PUBLISHING HISTORY
Jove edition / January 2013

Copyright © 2012 by Penguin Group (USA) Inc.
Cover illustration by Milo Sinovcic.

ISBN: 978-0-515-15127-5

JOVE®
Jove Books are published by The Berkley Publishing Group,
a division of Penguin Group (USA) Inc.,
375 Hudson Street, New York, New York 10014.
JOVE® is a registered trademark of Penguin Group (USA) Inc.
The "J" design is a trademark of Penguin Group (USA) Inc.

PRINTED IN THE UNITED STATES OF AMERICA

10 9 8 7 6 5 4 3 2 1

ALWAYS LEARNING   **PEARSON**

Chapter 1

Deputy United States Marshal Custis Long wasn't looking forward to meeting the newly hired deputy that wintery Denver morning as he headed for the Federal Building on Colfax Avenue. Not that he was unfriendly or hostile to the new men that his boss hired but, dammit, why did it always fall to him to have to take the department's recruits under his wing and teach them the dangerous business of being a professional lawman? Half of the new hires didn't last a month when they discovered that the low wages of a deputy didn't begin to compensate for the dangers and twenty-four-hour-a-day demands of the job.

"Good morning, Marshal," a city officer said, tipping his hat. "Think that this winter will ever give up and go away?"

Longarm was about to reply when he slipped on a patch of icy sidewalk and did a very ungainly flop.

"Uggh!" he grunted, hauling himself erect. "You

know, I don't mind the cold too much, and even the snow is fine . . . but this damnable ice is what I especially hate."

"I know," the Denver policeman said with a sympathetic shake of his head. "I've been out here since six o'clock this morning, and I've already seen four others besides you step on that patch of ice and do a hard fall."

"How about asking the city to put some cinders or salt down on the sidewalks so people don't break their necks trying to get to their work?"

"City is almost broke as usual. Hell, not a week goes by that I'm not worried about whether or not they will pay me." The man whose name Longarm now recalled being Tom Sullivan managed a smile and blew a cloud of steam into his gloved hands. "I'll bet the temperature got down to zero last night. I heard that there was a fire about midnight over near Cherry Creek and the fire wagon couldn't so much as put out a spit of water because their tank was frozen solid! Place burned to the ground."

"It's late February," Longarm said, slapping the snow and ice off his coat and pants. "This winter will soon be over."

"Don't bet on it," Officer Sullivan countered. "I've seen it snow here in March."

"Yeah, I know," Longarm said. "But see if you can get something done about this icy sidewalk before someone breaks bones or cracks open their skull."

"It'll start to melt in a few more hours," Sullivan promised. "But I'll try to warn people."

"Well," Longarm snapped with irritation, "you sure didn't warn me."

"Thought you'd see it and walk around."

Longarm frowned and continued up the street. When he arrived at the Federal Building, he ascended stairs to the second floor, where his office was located.

"Marshal Vail is waiting for you with the new man," one of the officers said.

"How's he looking?"

"Vail or the new man?"

"The new man."

The officer shrugged. "He looks like a boy. I doubt he even needs to shave yet. And get this.. . . his father is our *mayor*."

Longarm blinked. "What . . ."

The officer shrugged and went back to reading his newspaper, saying, "Don't ask me anything. All I know is that this one is a real peach and you had better treat him right or you'll soon have your nuts crushed in a political vise."

Longarm's already dark mood grew a shade darker. "Why on earth would Billy Vail hire the *mayor's* son!"

The officer glanced up from his morning paper. "Dunno. I expect that he had no choice."

"Yeah, just like I don't have any choice in taking him on," Longarm growled as he headed toward Billy's office.

"Come in!" Billy said, rising to his feet behind his desk. "Marshal Long, I'd like you to meet our new deputy, Henry Plummer."

Longarm turned to see a man, who looked to be no more than twenty, with rosy cheeks and a wide, infectious smile, extend his hand. Longarm managed a smile and shook Henry's hand, which was soft but at least had a firm grip. "How are you doin' today, Henry?"

"I'm fine," Plummer said. "I feel honored to finally meet you, Marshal Long. I've heard so much about you for years."

"Some good, I hope."

"All good," Plummer said enthusiastically. "And Marshal Vail says that you've kindly offered to take me under your wing and show me the ropes, so to speak."

Longarm was very tempted to tell the new man that he hadn't "offered" anything but had been ordered to take on the new man. "I expect that we'll just do some routine work, Henry. Nothing much out of the ordinary."

But Billy Vail had a different idea. "Truth is, Custis, I've got something pretty special for you and Henry to work on this week. Something not too dangerous but interesting."

Longarm studied his boss for a minute and said, "I thought you said that I had to get my backlog of paperwork taken care of this week."

"Aw," Billy said expansively, "that can wait awhile longer. I have something much more pressing for you and young Marshal Plummer. Why don't you both sit down and we'll talk about it."

"I'm all ears," Longarm said drily as he cast an appraising glance at the new recruit, noting that Henry Plummer was almost as tall as himself but much lighter in weight. He was a remarkably good-looking fellow with sandy-blond hair, deep blue eyes, and perfect teeth that gave him a boyish look, which was not a good thing for a federal marshal. When a lawman went up against some of the Denver hard cases that he was sure to face off against, it always helped to have a tough appearance rather than one that was overly friendly and youthful. Henry was also too well dressed for his new career. His suit and pants had obviously been expensively tailored, and his gold watch put Longarm's railroad watch and chain to shame. Henry's boots were shined to a high polish, and Longarm would have bet anything that Henry had not ever shined his own boots but instead paid for the service.

"So, Henry, why don't you tell us all a little about yourself before we talk business," Billy Vail suggested. "I know your father quite well and he's doing a fine job as mayor."

"Thank you," Henry said, looking genuinely pleased. "I'll pass that compliment on to him."

"So," Longarm said, already getting impatient with the niceties of this conversation. "Why did you decide that you wanted to be a federal marshal when I'm sure that you could have done many things that were less dangerous and paid more money?"

"Oh," Henry said, giving him a self-deprecating shrug and smile, "I just wanted to do something different than my father and his friends. Mostly, I wanted to be a lawman and prove to myself that I could handle danger and take responsibility. You know, be my own man."

"If you don't mind my asking, why do you think," Longarm said choosing his words with care, "that becoming a law officer is the only way that you can become your 'own man'?"

For the first time, Henry Plummer dropped his

amicable act and looked first at Billy and then directly into Longarm's eyes. All the pretend good humor went right out of him. "Do you know anything about my family?"

"Only that your father made a fortune in real estate somewhere back east and then got into politics and has done pretty well here, too."

"My father lost my mother when I was only six years old," Henry Plummer said in a subdued voice. "Back then my parents lived in Baltimore, and before my father inherited some money and began investing in real estate he was a local policeman."

Longarm was caught by surprise. "Your father was once a policeman?"

"A highly decorated detective in Baltimore," Plummer said proudly.

"That's right," Billy said, sitting up straighter. "I'd forgotten reading about that part of the mayor's distinguished background some years ago."

"Well maybe you also read how my mother . . . was murdered." Henry Plummer bent his head and took a deep breath. "She was only twenty-seven at the time."

"I don't believe that I read anything about that," Billy admitted.

"My mother was taking me to a private school just two blocks from our home. She was beautiful, and I suppose it was obvious that we had some money even back in those days. So when two hard cases accosted her demanding her purse and jewelry, it must have seemed to them to be an easy mark."

Longarm threw a leg over his knee and leaned forward because this story wasn't expected and it was getting interesting.

"Go on," Billy urged.

"Everything went wrong in seconds," Henry Plummer whispered, his voice now strained with emotion. "A local police officer happened to see what was going on and came running to our aid. He pulled a revolver, but he couldn't possibly fire at the two thieves, for fear of hitting either myself or my mother. Knowing that full well, the two men also shot the Baltimore policeman to death right in the middle of the street. When my mother tried to stop them, they turned and one of the men shot her point-blank in the heart. Two bullets, dead center."

Henry Plummer stopped, momentarily unable to continue.

After a pause, Longarm said, "Henry, you don't have to say anything more."

"Oh," Henry said, "but I do. When my mother fell to the street, she was choking and quivering in the throes, and I told her that I would one day find those two men and bring them to justice and then I would make it my life's work to take people like that off the streets. The moment she died, I ran to the policeman's side but he was already gone. The man wasn't much older than my mother and left a wife and two children."

"That was quite a thing for a six-year-old boy to have to go through," Longarm said quietly. "And I'm sorry you had to see your mother and that brave law officer cut down before your eyes."

"I am, too," Billy Vail said.

"You haven't quite heard the end of the story," Henry whispered. "Those men were identified but never caught. For years, my father tried to track them down and make them pay for the terrible thing that they had done to my mother and the Baltimore officer. But they always seemed to be just beyond the grasp of the law. They moved from city to city, never staying more than a few months and always robbing and killing innocent people. As I was growing up, justice was all that my father talked about, until the last detective he hired confirmed that the pair were brothers and that they had finally put roots down here in Denver. As a law officer, I mean to find them and get even."

"Do you know their names?"

"Yeah. Dirk and Harold Raney. At least that was what they used to be called. "My father is pretty sure that they changed their names when they got to Denver, because he hired a detective here and the man came up empty-handed."

"What did they do to make a living besides robbing people?"

"They were pickpockets and petty thieves. I think one or maybe both were mule skinners and freight wagon drivers."

Longarm glanced sharply at his boss, who said, "Listen, Henry, perhaps I made a mistake in swearing you in as an officer. And while I'm sure that Custis as well as I, we're deeply saddened by what happened when you were six years old . . . well, this isn't the place for you or your father to see your long overdue restitution."

"I think it is exactly the place for that," Henry

Plummer bluntly told them. "I made that solemn childhood vow to my dying mother and I mean to keep it or die trying."

Longarm stood up. "Billy, we need to talk privately for a few moments *right now*."

"Sure," Billy said, looking very grim. "Henry, would you please step outside?"

"All right, but I need to tell you that I'm not someone obsessed by revenge or gaining restitution. I'll treat even criminals with respect, and I'm going to be an asset to your department, if you'll just give me a fair chance."

"Thank you for saying that," Billy told the earnest young man. "But I still need for you to step outside for a moment."

Henry Plummer looked straight into Longarm's eyes. "I know that you and Marshal Vail are disturbed by my story, I had to tell it. Believe me that I thought long and hard about revealing to you the tragedy of my childhood . . . but I determined that I had to be completely honest with you even if it meant losing this job before it began."

"I respect that," Longarm told the young man. "Just give us a few minutes."

"Of course."

Once they were alone, Billy spoke first. "Custis, I fear that I've made a huge mistake by hiring young Plummer. I didn't know anything about him other than that he was our mayor's son. I had met him a time or two at social occasions and always thought he was forthright and upstanding. A young man with real character, and you know how much I respect his father and the work he is doing to help and improve our city."

"Yes, I've also met the mayor, and he's a fine man, but Billy, I'm not too sure about hiring Henry Plummer. He seems honest and sincere, but what if this is just his way of trying to get at those two who murdered his mother and that policeman back in Baltimore?"

"Would that be such a bad thing?" Billy asked.

"It would be if he intends to exact his own restitution on them. Billy, you know that if he should find that pair and use this office as an excuse for an execution, it will fall heavily on your shoulders, and stain this department's sterling reputation forever."

"I know."

Billy rested his chin on his hand and closed his eyes for a moment as he considered his difficult decision. Finally, he opened his eyes and said, "Custis, I'd like to give Henry a chance at being a good lawman, and you're the best man that I can think of to help me do that. However, if you feel in your heart this is all going to go bad on us and the department, then say so and I'll ask Henry Plummer to resign."

"I'd prefer to give Henry Plummer a fair chance."

"Then it's settled," Billy decided.

He opened the door and called his new recruit back inside. Henry looked a bit pale, and strain was very evident on his handsome young face. "Well," he asked, "what is the verdict?"

"I'm not going to ask you to resign," Billy told him. "But I am going to make you give us a promise."

"What kind of promise?"

"That you'll never use this office to justify executing those two men if ever you can find them, and that you will always follow my orders and those of Deputy Marshal Custis Long to the letter."

"I agree," Henry Plummer said quickly. "I swear to you that I will follow your orders."

"And not focus your attention on finding those two murderers from Baltimore and killing them?" Longarm asked.

"Yes, I agree to that. But . . ."

"Then," Longarm said quickly, "we'll team up and see if we can do some damage on the lawless element in this fair city."

"That suits me right down to the ground," Henry declared. "When can we get started?"

Marshal Billy Vail motioned for his most experienced marshal and his most inexperienced to have a seat. "Now that we've cleared the air and settled that other matter," he said officiously, "let me tell you about a small band of thugs who are terrorizing the population down at the South End of this city and have robbed two federal banks, and how I think we can put a stop to them once and for all."

"Sounds like fun," Longarm said, relaxing as he turned to look at his new partner. "What do you think, Henry?"

"I can't wait to get started."

"Oh," Longarm said, "by the way, did Marshal Vail even ask you if you knew how to use a gun?"

Henry pulled out a two-shot derringer. "I can hit something close with this, and I'm pretty handy with my fists. My father insisted that I take boxing lessons so that I would never be bullied. I am very fast, have an excellent right cross and a stiff left jab. But my favorite punch is an uppercut to the solar plexus."

"Your hands are clean and your face is unscarred," Longarm said. "It's hard for me to believe you've ever taken a hard punch."

"That's right," Plummer said. "I've been schooled in the art of self-defense. I can duck, bob, and weave, and no one has ever really been able to hit me."

Longarm and Billy exchanged dubious glances.

"That's all well and good," Longarm said, "but I'm talking about weapons that shoot *bullets*. And a derringer is hardly what I was referring to. What I want to know is if you are a good pistol or rifle shot."

Henry Plummer took a sudden interest in the floor. He didn't have to answer the question. Longarm knew that he was greener than grass and would have to be taught everything from scratch.

Chapter 2

Longarm and newly hired Deputy Henry Plummer left the Federal Building an hour later and walked briskly up the snowy street. When they came to where Officer Tom Sullivan was standing, the local policeman yelled, "Hey, Custis, want to show me how to take another big fall? Maybe this time you could do a complete somersault!"

"Up yours, Sullivan!"

"Ha! You took the most entertaining fall of the morning. Good to see you back on these icy streets."

Longarm shot the man a hard stare and then made a wide detour of the icy patch. They still hadn't put any salt or cinders on it, and he had the feeling that had the city done so, they would have robbed Officer Sullivan of his sole entertainment.

"What was that all about?" Deputy Plummer asked.

"Never mind. You'll soon learn that there is some resentment and jealousy from the local officers toward us federal officers."

"Why?"

"We get paid better and have more interesting jobs. Did you ask your father to have the city hire you as a local constable out on a beat?"

"Never entered my mind to stand on the street directing traffic all day and hoping to catch some petty thief or pickpocket."

"Does your father ever miss being a Baltimore detective?"

"Nope. He's doing what he thinks is important and trying to make this a better and safer city."

"I admire him for that," Longarm said. "Politics is a rough-and-tumble game with no holds barred."

Henry Plummer switched the conversation. "How are we going to get enough evidence to arrest an entire gang of thieves and bank robbers?"

"Not sure," Longarm admitted. "My mode of operation is to go right to the problem, study it a little, and then take the appropriate action. Right now we don't even have any names, and we've got no idea exactly how many are in this gang. What we do know is that they operate out of a certain part of the city and they have guns but have yet to use them in their crimes."

"But you'd have to assume that they would kill if necessary."

"That's right," Longarm agreed. "I always take the stance that the men who break the law are capable of killing me without a moment's hesitation. I've known some lawmen who gave criminals the benefit of doubt. Good lawmen that fell for a line of malarkey or a sob story and paid for it with their lives. I trust none of the men who cross the line and break the law. Some are just desperate, some stupid, some insane, and some filled with more hatred than you can imagine."

"I hate the brothers that murdered my mother and that officer back when I was a little boy."

"I know and don't blame you. The thing of it is," Longarm said, "hatred can either work for . . . or against you."

"What do you mean?"

"If you hate someone but keep it under control, you can use the emotion to bring them to justice, knowing that putting them behind bars for a long while or even sending them to the hangman's gallows is the best kind of restitution or revenge."

"You really believe that it's the 'best kind'?"

"I do," Longarm said with assurance. "Have you ever been to a prison where the worst of the worst are sent?"

"No."

"Then I'll take you out to our state prison. It turns convicts into tortured men . . . men who stare into space and see no future, no happiness, and most importantly no hope. Some live for years in cells not much larger than Billy's little office. They pace the stone floors, pound the brick walls, and scream until they either go mad or fall down sobbing like spanked children."

Henry Plummer walked along in silence for several minutes, until he blurted, "But I've heard that some of them grow even stronger with their hatred of the law and of society."

"That's true. But even as they become ever more hateful, they become ever more frustrated and crazed.

Believe me, Henry, a life sentence without any possibility of parole in a hard prison is a far worse fate than any hangman's noose."

"If that's true, I still feel no satisfaction. My mother and that brave officer in Baltimore who died in the line of duty had their precious gifts of life taken away forever. The two brothers who shot them are still living."

"Maybe and maybe not. But if we find them and send them to prison for the rest of their days, then their lives will have no hope or pleasure at all."

"I suppose you're right." Henry Plummer watched Longarm remove his badge and place it in his pocket while still in full stride.

"Why are you doing that?"

"In the neighborhood that we're about to enter they have been known to ambush lawmen on sight."

Henry's head shot around and he stared at all the buildings, most now derelict and abandoned in the hard neighborhood that they were entering. "But can't they tell by looking at us that we're law officers?"

"Probably."

"Then what's the point in hiding our badges?"

"Maybe there is no point," Longarm conceded. "But all the same I still like to keep a low profile and just get deeper into this neighborhood. Put your badge in your pocket, Henry."

"So we just come out here to this shabby part of town and walk around?"

"We don't 'just walk around,' " Longarm said pointedly. "We go to places where men drink and their loose talk . . . after we buy them some drinks . . . can give us valuable information."

"We pay to get them *drunk*?" Henry asked with distaste.

"Works for me and unless you have a better idea of how to get information, then that's what we're going to do." Longarm pointed to a saloon that was notorious for fights, stabbings, shootings, and general mayhem. "This is where we start. When we go inside, we don't try to attract any attention but just sidle up to the bar and order beer. We stand and we drink a glass or two, and then we look around and decide if there are people inside who might be helpful."

"And if they are around and don't try to kill us first?"

"We buy them whiskey. Lots and lots of cheap whiskey."

They stopped and stood out in the cold and grimy street for several moments. Henry looked nervous. "Custis, I sure didn't imagine this was going to be how a federal officer of the law operates."

"If you don't like it . . . then leave," Longarm said flatly.

"You should know that I'm not much of a drinker."

"That could change if you keep this job. But for now the beer we'll be served is so green and foul that you aren't likely to be tempted to do more than sip it."

"All right," Henry Plummer agreed. "I'll go along with this and do my best to learn."

"That's the spirit," Longarm said, pushing open the door of the dimly lit saloon and heading straight for the bar. "Just keep your eyes open and your mouth shut and we might do just fine in here."

"And if we don't?"

Longarm didn't have to think twice to come up with his answer. "Then we fight our way out and head for another saloon."

"Wonderful," Henry said cryptically as Longarm sidled up to the scarred and rickety bar and called for the bartender to bring them a couple of beers.

The bartender certainly didn't bust his butt hurrying to get them served. He looked around at the dozen or so customers nursing their drinks, and his face said that he wished the two lawmen had gone to some place else to drink . . . any place else for that matter.

"Marshal Long," the bartender whispered as he set two mugs in front of them. "I haven't seen you in here since you beat Charlie Epp with a pistol and sent Billy Montgomery to the hospital with two broken arms and then arrested three of my best customers."

"Yeah, that happened this past spring." Longarm took a sip of his beer and grimaced. "Still serving the same pig piss, huh?"

"You don't like it, then leave."

"Aw," Longarm snorted, "I'm thirsty, so I'll finish my beer. Have you missed me, Johnny?"

"Like a case of the measles." Johnny glanced at Longarm's companion. With a contemptuous sneer he asked, "Babysitting this afternoon are we, Marshal Long?"

Before Longarm could reply, Henry Plummer shot out a straight left fist across the top of the bar and poked the bartender in the eye, knocking him back into a wall of bottles.

"Damn!" Longarm said, restraining his new deputy. "What the hell is the matter with you?"

"I told you I had a good left jab. What I forgot to mention is that I won't take being bullied or insulted."

The bartender shook his head. "Kid, you had better get the hell out of this saloon before I . . ."

"Before you what?" Longarm asked in a low voice. "Shoot a United States deputy marshal down in cold blood?"

Johnny gingerly touched his swelling eye. "He had no right to do that!"

"I think Deputy Plummer had every right to pop you in the eye . . . which, by the way, is already starting to swell shut. If you have any ice handy, I'd put some on it to keep down the swelling. Or you could just go outside and break an icicle."

Johnny was a big man, and Longarm had heard that he was also a dangerous, hard-fighting, two-fisted brawler who could more than hold his own with his oftentimes rowdy customers.

"I ever see you around when Marshal Long isn't at your side for protection," Johnny warned, "I'll rearrange that pretty face."

Henry Plummer didn't appear to be in the least bit intimidated. "Big talk. Why don't you remove that momma's apron and come outside so we can see how fast I can shut that other eye. Come on!"

Johnny started to whip off his apron, and some of the bar's customers looked eagerly toward the door, hoping to see Johnny pound the young deputy to a bloody pulp.

"Enough!" Longarm snapped. "Johnny, you insulted my friend and got what you deserved."

"I didn't deserve shit!"

"How about I buy you and the house a round of whiskey and we just let things settle down a mite?" Longarm calmly suggested. "No point in me having to bust your place up and send you to jail . . . is there?"

Johnny swore. "All right, I'll simmer down. Fact is that I didn't even see the punch coming. The kid hits hard and fast."

"I'm accurate, too," Henry said. "I could have hit you in the throat and put you down for the count . . . but I didn't."

"If you're expecting any thanks you can kiss my ass," Johnny snapped before he turned toward his other customers and shouted, "Drinks are on the house!"

The stampede to the bar was both immediate and impressive. Johnny filled every man's dirty glass to the brim, using up two entire bottles of whiskey. "This is gonna cost you, Marshal. I just hope that your young friend and I meet outside someday."

"I'd like that, too," Henry Plummer said. "And you can take this piss you call beer and toss it in the shitter. I'll have some whiskey along with everyone else."

Longarm looked suspiciously at his companion. "Easy does it, Henry," he whispered. "The thing you have to remember is that you get other people drunk, but you don't ever get drunk yourself."

"Well hellfire! That sure doesn't sound like much fun to me!" Henry's face was flushed, and he hooked his thumbs into his vest pockets and crowed, "Is everyone in this pigsty happy?"

Longarm watched Henry Plummer toss back his glass of whiskey, pound it down on the table, and motion for seconds.

"Uh-uh," Longarm said, voice hardening as he knocked the glass spinning across the bar and into the dirty sawdust on the floor. "You weren't fooling when you said you weren't much of a drinker."

"But you told me that would probably change because of this job!"

"It won't change if you wind up dead the first time out," Longarm growled. "Now, you've had enough to drink, so sober up and stay alert."

Henry Plummer made the sound of flatulence, and then he giggled.

Jaysus, Longarm thought, *the mayor's kid is already drunk on his damned feet!*

Chapter 3

Longarm bought a second round of whiskey, figuring that his boss wouldn't be too upset when he sought reimbursement. By then it was getting well into the afternoon and the saloon was starting to get real busy. So far, no one had approached the pair of federal lawmen, but Longarm knew that would change soon enough.

"How long do we have to stand here and wait before something happens?" Plummer griped, looking red-eyed and hungover. "Waiting in this shit hole has grown old in a hurry."

"Patience is one of the most important virtues of a good lawman. Didn't your father ever tell you that, given that he was a detective?"

"He never once told me that part of being a lawman was to stand around buying drinks in a lousy, stinking saloon."

"Well, the next time you see him, ask him about

my methods, and I'll be interested to hear his comments."

"Hey."

Longarm turned to see a thin, ragged, and unshaven man about his own age standing with an empty glass in his hand. "Yeah?"

He leaned forward, smelling like a sewer. "Don't you even remember me? Monty Higgins?"

"No. Should I?"

"Yeah. You arrested me about four years ago for trying to rob a bank. I botched the job, only got about ten dollars, and after I was caught, I went to prison for a couple of years."

"You break the law and you pay the price," Longarm said, edging off the bar and putting a little more distance between himself and the filthy man. "You have an issue with me for doing my job?"

"Nah," Higgins said. "I deserved what I got." He looked around Longarm to stare at Henry Plummer. "Who the hell is *he*?"

"He's a marshal same as I am."

"Looks like a choirboy."

"You got anything important to tell me, Monty?"

Monty had a few drinks in him and made quite a show out of pretending to look around to see if anyone was paying attention. "Not in here, I don't. You buy me a full bottle of whiskey and meet me around behind the saloon and we can talk."

"Someone has been robbing banks and doing a better job than you ever did at it," Longarm said in a low voice. "We hear they've also been terrorizing people in this neighborhood."

Monty took a furtive glance over his shoulder and then whispered, "Out back in thirty minutes. Bring a bottle of Old Barrelhead and leave the choirboy here."

"I'll think about it," Longarm said, turning away from the man.

When Monty disappeared, Henry Plummer asked, "Is that really the kind of man that you'd trust to help us?"

"Yeah. He's a drunk and he's desperate. Monty also knows that I'll send him straight back to prison if he leads us astray."

Plummer shook his head. "I don't like this . . . not any of it."

"Then give me your badge and get the hell out of here," Longarm said, not bothering to hide his irritation.

"Too soon. Right now it's in for a penny, in for a pound."

"You can quit anytime you want," Longarm told the green deputy. "I won't brook any insolence or interference. We play it my way or you are out."

"I'm still in."

"Good. Stay sober when I'm gone."

Ten minutes later, Longarm was in the back alley with a bottle. When Monty reached for it, Longarm shook his head. "I'm not St. Nicholas and you're not getting a Christmas present. Tell me what you have and I'll decide if it's worth what you've asked to be paid."

Monty took a ragged breath. They were in the deep shadows of the nearby buildings, surrounded by garbage and the powerful stench of piss and shit. Flies buzzed frantically, and it wasn't a place where anyone wanted to linger and talk about the weather.

Although they were clearly the only ones in the alley, Monty leaned closer and whispered. "They call themselves the Shamrock Gang."

" 'Shamrock'?"

"Yeah. They're mostly Irish toughs. Some have jobs, some don't. They play rough and for keeps."

"How many? And give me the names of their leaders."

"I don't *know* how many," Monty replied. "They move about, and I don't think that they're ever all in one place at one time. Their leader is supposed to be a man named Bully O'Brien."

"You've seen him?"

"Oh, yeah. He's a big, mean bastard with a busted nose and a quick temper. He's missing most of an ear and has an ugly scar across one eyelid. People walk way around Bully O'Brien."

"Was he in that saloon?"

Monty shook his head vigorously. "Hell no! Do you take me for a complete idiot?"

"Give me some more names."

"There is Crazy Mick O'Toole and Bad Barry Hannigan. Those are the main ones to worry about."

"Where do they live?"

"All over this neighborhood."

Longarm considered this information and thought he had heard of all these men, so maybe Monty was telling him the truth. "Is there any way that I can spot them before they spot me?"

"No. But I'll tell you this much, Marshal. Any one of them would slit your throat for a mug of green beer."

"What else can you tell me?"

"That's it." Monty licked his lips and ran his hand across his dirty stubble of a beard. "Marshal, I got to get out of here. Someone could be watching us right now!"

"We're in deep shadows."

"Yeah, but they might have seen us round the corner and come back here. Come on! Give me that bottle and let me get away from you. I did my part of the deal."

Longarm could see that Monty was starting to get real nervous. "All right," he said, handing over the bottle. "Do you know where the Federal Building is located?"

"Sure. Everyone does."

"I work with the deputy I was with on the second floor. If you can get me any good information, come by and I'll pay you fairly for your trouble."

Monty yanked the cork off the bottle and upended it. He took a long, shuddering gulp and choked, "I'll keep that in mind."

Monty was gone before Longarm could say anything more. He waited five minutes and then started out of the alley. Just as he was about to get to the street in front of the saloon, he heard a shriek followed by a strangled cry and then the sound of a bottle shattering on cobblestones.

Longarm carried his Colt revolver on his left hip, butt forward. He drew it and jumped forward to see a man in a dark overcoat disappear around a corner, running hard, while in his wake lay Monty Higgins facedown, toes dancing on the dirty sidewalk.

"Monty!"

Longarm knelt in a spreading pool of blood and turned the ex-convict over. That's when he saw that Monty had gotten his throat cut from ear to ear. The poor bastard was gurgling and shaking, and his blood gushing was like a park fountain.

Longarm's head snapped up and the murderer was gone. When he looked back down at Monty, the ex-convict was gone, too.

Longarm and Plummer had summoned people to come and collect Monty's body. There wasn't anything on it to pass on to relatives or even friends.

"He had *nothing*," Henry Plummer said as they entered the Federal Building.

"That's right," Longarm agreed. "Monty Higgins rolled the dice and lost."

"Because of us."

"His choice, Henry." Longarm looked at his shaken companion, who seemed to have aged dramatically since they'd first met that very same morning. "Why don't you go home and we'll start fresh in the morning."

"I'm not sure I want to wait until morning."

"I need to think this out," Longarm told the new hire. "Plan a strategy."

"What's to plan? We go back to that neighborhood, find those men, and either arrest or kill them."

"And you think it's just that easy?"

"Why not?"

"Get out of here and come back early tomorrow morning. We'll do something then."

"But . . ."

"Go!"

Deputy Plummer's face flushed with anger and his lips drew tight at the corners, but he said nothing as he stomped back out of the building.

Longarm glanced toward Billy's office, saw that it was empty, and decided that he would call it a day himself. There was blood on the knees of his trousers, and he felt tired, dirty, and depressed. He had wanted his first day with the new man to be a good one, and it could hardly have been worse. Now, as he headed for his room, he wondered if Monty had even given him real names . . . or just ones made up so that he could get the bottle of cheap whiskey.

Irene Wilson was checking her mail when Longarm entered the foyer of his modest rooming house. "My gawd, Custis, you look awful!"

"Thanks."

"I'm sorry. Listen, Custis, I've got a full bottle of pretty good whiskey and a strong shoulder to cry on. Interested?"

"I might be after I clean up."

"Come join me for a while and we'll talk."

Longarm dredged up a smile. "Irene, I'm not sure that *talk* is what I need."

Irene winked. His new landlady was in her mid-thirties, had shapely legs, a small waist, and long brown hair. By any man's standard, she was good-looking, and she never tried to put hooks into a man when he was down or in dire need of some comfort.

Irene was the manager of a local grocery store, and she also made a little extra money and accepted gifts from a few favorite men . . . Longarm being one of them. She wasn't the marrying kind, and she usually sold the gifts that Longarm gave her or pawned them, without the pretense of sentiment. Irene didn't like children but had three cats in her own rooms, and she had an unusually bawdy sense of humor.

What more could a man like Longarm ask for after such a rotten day?

Forty minutes later, Longarm was drinking quality whiskey and undressing in Irene's bedroom.

"It's pretty obvious that you're in a hurry this time," Irene said, tossing down a shot. "Usually, you like to talk a little first and let us work up to a good romp."

"I've done about as much talking as I can stand for one day, Irene. Are you good with that or maybe I should . . ."

"Shut up and finish undressing. It hasn't been all that great of a day for me, either."

He finished undressing and watched her do the same. But he was a curious man and had to ask, "So what went wrong with your day?"

"First thing this morning I stepped on a patch of ice and really took a hard spill. That big Irish palooka cop saw it and burst out laughing."

"Tom Sullivan."

"Yeah. He really made me mad! Even madder than I was for stepping on that ice and falling."

"I'm going to figure out some way to get him," Longarm decided out loud. "Something that will teach

Officer Sullivan that people don't like to be laughed at when they take a bad spill."

"Well," Irene said, "when you figure out how to do that, let me know and I'll be in on it all the way." She turned around and made a pose. "I'll bet you see a big, purple bruise on my butt, huh?"

Irene had a very shapely butt and it was noticeably bruised. "It still looks good to me, Honey. But for the sake of your comfort, I'll go easy on it."

"You'd better not!" Irene flopped down on her bed, spread her long legs, and motioned him to join her. "Come on, Custis, let's do a little doggie and pony and have some fun. Make us both forget about what wasn't a very good day."

Longarm would never tell Irene about his recent staring down at the gaping slash in Monty's neck and seeing the light die in the man's terrified eyes. Nope. That kind of thing a person in his profession learned to keep to himself. Irene might have had a bad day, but she would be shocked to learn how really bad Longarm's day had been.

"Why, Custis!" she cried with surprise. "You're not completely hard yet."

He looked down at his manhood and flushed with embarrassment. "Damn, what is wrong with me?"

"Nothing Irene can't fix real quick. Come here."

Longarm came to her, and she took his flaccid manhood in her mouth and began to make him feel very special. In less than a minute he was long and hard, and the terrible and gruesome vision that had been plaguing his mind was gone and replaced by raw desire.

"Well that big, hairy thing is sure looking a lot more healthy," Irene said, taking him out of her mouth and studying him like a laboratory specimen. "I think it might actually be up to the moment now. What do you think?"

"Irene, you're just what the doctor ordered," Long-arm growled as he mounted his friend and his neighbor. He pulled those legs up, and she locked them around his hips with her ankles.

Irene kissed his face, then his lips, while he rutted on her like a lust-crazed pagan. She began to make little mewing sounds, then louder woman sounds, then after a while she let out a wail like a big she-cat on top of a mountain.

Longarm roared and filled her with his seed. Soon after, they sat naked, backs resting against Irene's bed, tins of sardines in their hands, cracker crumbs scattered—all while they munched and drank whiskey, finally feeling happy and content.

"Irene," he said, "you are one hell of a woman."

"Glad you finally noticed," she told him. "You gonna want to do it to me again soon?"

"Soon as I finish this can of sardines."

She looked at him intently and then shocked him by asking, "Do I smell like sardines down between my legs?"

When he recovered, he replied, "Not that I remember."

"Maybe you forgot and need to find out if I do."

"Jeez, Irene, you're always wanting more."

"Yeah, just like you." She laughed, biting his chest

and then popping a drippy sardine into her lovely mouth.

Later that evening, Irene laid her head on his chest. "Something really rotten happened to you today, didn't it?"

"Pretty bad."

"I saw the bloodstains on your pants. Want to talk about it?"

"Nope."

"Might help."

He kissed her tenderly. "If I thought it would help me and not hurt you, I'd talk. But I think that would be a mistake."

"You don't want to upset me," she said. "That's because you really care about me, don't you?"

"Yeah, Irene. I really, really do."

Chapter 4

Longarm overslept the next morning and didn't get to the office until well after nine o'clock. Billy Vail and Henry Plummer were both impatiently waiting.

"Well, well, if it isn't Custis Long. My, but I'm glad you had a full night's sleep," Billy said caustically. "Hope this job isn't cramping your night life too much."

Longarm couldn't stand it when his boss got sarcastic. "Stow it, Billy."

"Both of you come into my office." It was clear by the tone of Billy Vail's voice that this wasn't going to be a friendly chat.

"Close the door and take your seats," Billy ordered, then asked, "Custis, guess what happened to me early this morning?"

"Your dog barfed on your bed?"

"No! I was awakened at five o'clock this morning by a Denver policeman and informed that the chief of police requested that I come to his office *immediately*."

"Billy, you sure as hell don't work for him," Longarm said. "You should have told the officer to send the chief of police over to *this* office at a reasonable hour."

"I try very hard to always to keep a friendly and open relationship with the locals," Billy snapped. "So I went over to the man's office and guess what I learned?"

"I think I can guess," Longarm mused. "You got a full report about us and how a man named Monty Higgins had his throat cut outside the saloon we were drinking at."

"That's right!" Billy exploded. "So instead of my deputies filing a report late yesterday afternoon, they both took off and I knew nothing until I was reamed out by the local authorities!"

"It's my fault," Longarm confessed. "Henry and I were trying to get some information about that gang, and I think that we did."

Billy relaxed and managed a thin smile. "Well, that would be nice. Tell me what you learned, so that I can feel better about having gotten chewed out at seven o'clock this morning."

Longarm wasn't fully awake. He and Irene had perhaps overindulged a little, both in the flesh and in the drink. "Henry, why don't you fill our boss in while I get a cup of coffee?"

"You stay right where you are, Custis!" Billy ordered. "All right, Deputy Plummer, tell me some good news."

"Mr. Higgins told Custis that the criminal in charge of the Shamrock Gang is named Bully O'Brien and that his main henchmen are Crazy Mick O'Toole and Bad Barry Harrigan."

"I'm pretty sure that I've heard of them all," Billy said. "But, if my memory serves me well, that bunch has always been petty thieves, thugs, and intimidators. I can't imagine them daring to rob banks."

"Well," Plummer said, "apparently they do."

"Hmmm." Billy drummed his fingers on his desk for a few moments and then said, "How should we handle this, Custis?"

"I think we need to send someone into that area that is Irish and looks like he is a wanted man on the run. Someone tough and dirty that won't arouse suspicion. He can spend a week gathering information and then we go after that bunch in force and round them all up at once."

Billy nodded. "Makes sense."

"I volunteer to be the wanted man," Henry Plummer said quickly.

"No good," Longarm told everyone. "You've already been seen with me at that saloon. Perhaps if you hadn't popped Johnny the bartender in the eye, no one would remember you if you were dressed poorly and unshaven. But you did and he'll remember you, no matter what your disguise."

"You punched Johnny?" Billy Vail asked. "I've heard he's a tough and dangerous man."

"He insulted me," Henry Plummer said, trying to look contrite.

"Even so," Billy said. "You're now a sworn officer of the law, and a verbal insult is hardly sufficient provocation to strike a citizen. Even one who provokes you with insults. Use physical force *only* when necessary."

"Yes, sir."

"Custis, you're going to have to start teaching young Henry a few things about what we can and can't do while we wear a badge."

"We took our badges off before we went into that saloon," Henry Plummer explained.

"What!"

Longarm had heard enough. "Look, Billy, I have my own way of doing things and I've been pretty successful for a long time, haven't I?"

"Sure, but not wearing your badge and . . ."

"Why don't we talk about this later?" Longarm suggested. "Right now I think you should be focusing on who we can send into that south neighborhood and how we can make him look like a fugitive of the law."

"Yeah," Billy conceded, "you're right. The man we put in there is going to be risking his life from the start. He needs to be top-notch."

"How about Paddy Malloy?" Longarm suggested. "He's experienced and Irish."

"Paddy has a temper and he loves his drink a bit too much," Billy argued. "I'm not sure that he's the best man or that he'd get in and out without also having his throat cut."

"Then what about Mike Flannery?" Longarm suggested. "He's been with us for over a year. Mike is tough, determined, and smart."

"But he just got married," Billy said. "Be a crying shame if he was uncovered by this gang and murdered leaving a young widow."

"Yeah," Longarm said, "it would at that."

"But he's quite obviously the best man I have for this extremely dangerous job," Billy said quietly.

"Could you boys sort of back Deputy Flannery up without exposing his cover?"

"Of course," Longarm said. "It's not the thing that I do best . . . but I'm sure that Henry and I can figure out a way to stay close yet not too close. And Flannery looks like he stepped off the boat from Dublin."

"I'll see if he'll do it," Billy decided. "Henry, go get Deputy Flannery."

"I'm . . . I'm not sure who he is."

"Ask anyone. Mike isn't much older than you and he's full of blarney and bluster, but he's tough as boot leather."

As soon as Plummer was gone, Billy leaned forward on his desk. "Custis, I'm not sure that it's a good idea to hide your badge."

"It works well for me. The saloon we went into was filled with men who had been arrested and probably jailed or thrown into prison."

"Even so, the badge gives you *authority*."

"Look," Longarm said patiently, "why don't we just agree to disagree about this and see what Deputy Flannery has to say about putting his neck on the chopping block?"

Billy was about to say something more, when the two young deputies returned. Mike Flannery was of medium height and not especially strong or imposing physically, but Longarm had worked with the young man a few times and knew he was dedicated and fearless. He was also a little reckless and sometimes too loud, but he was smart enough to curb his exuberance when it counted. And Mike could shoot a gun and hit what he aimed at every time.

"Flannery, we have a job for you . . . if you want it."

"Whatever you say, Boss."

"This could be very dangerous, and you just got married to that beautiful girl, so I'm a little—"

"Marshal Vail," Flannery interrupted. "Delia knew when she married me that I was a law officer, and that meant that I would have to put my life on the line. She accepted that as part of the deal and she's fine about it. Delia is a woman, not a girl, and she understands the risks of my chosen profession. We talked about that plenty before we were even engaged."

"I see. In that case, have a seat, and we'll spell out what needs to be done and do a bit of planning on how to do it."

"I take it this is about the Shamrock Gang."

"That's right."

"I've heard they are a bad, bad bunch," Flannery said. "So whatever I can do to help would give me a great deal of satisfaction."

Longarm and Billy exchanged satisfied glances, both thinking that they had made the correct choice. "Custis, why don't you tell Billy what you and Deputy Plummer learned yesterday afternoon while drinking?"

Longarm explained everything to Mike Flannery and ended by saying, "We know who the leaders of this gang are, and we know they're brazen but probably very careful about who they mingle with. They're poor Irish and they're not only desperate, but extremely ruthless. They are the ones who slit that man's throat yesterday afternoon, and they'd do the same to yours if they discovered you were a federal officer."

"I understand."

"We need you to go into that neighborhood posing as a fugitive from the law."

"A man who escaped from prison or a jail?" Flannery asked.

"That would work fine. Or someone who has committed a serious crime and wasn't caught."

"Like murder."

"Murder would be good," Longarm said. "But you'd have to be very convincing, because your life will depend upon them believing you."

"I can do that," Deputy Flannery promised. "How long will I have to keep up the lie?"

"Good question," Billy said. "And there's no set answer. Keep it up only as long as it takes to get the ones that robbed the banks and who committed those other serious crimes. We're federal officers, of course, so the bank jobs are paramount to us, but I'm sure any other crimes that can be proven would be very interesting to the local authorities."

"You'll need to look rough," Longarm told the clean-shaven and respectable-looking lawman.

Flannery rubbed his square jaw. "My beard grows like a weed. By tomorrow I'll look as if I haven't shaved in a week. And as for the clothes and disguise, I know a few street drunks that will swap what I wear for what they wear and do so laughing their asses off."

Billy looked to Longarm to see if he had any more comments, and when Longarm did not, he said, "All right. Take the day off, grow your beard, enjoy the good company of your lovely new wife, get dirty and rough-looking, and we'll start tomorrow. Custis and Henry will work out the details and try to keep you protected."

"I'm up for it," Mike Flannery vowed. "Been doing paperwork for most of this month and I'm about to go stir-crazy at my desk."

"Good luck, and we'll see you all tomorrow morning at eight o'clock sharp. Got that, Custis?"

"Sure, Boss."

"Good. Then for the rest of today, maybe you could finally level that stack of reports that are overdue."

"Nothing I can think of would give me more pleasure," Longarm said cryptically before getting up and leaving.

"What would you like me to do today?" Henry Plummer asked his boss.

Billy thought about that a moment and said, "Why don't you tag along with Mike for a short time and see how he prepares for this one? Mike, that okay with you?"

"Sure."

Marshal Billy Vail watched his two young deputies leave and walk through the outer office. They were about the same age but could hardly be more different. Henry Plummer had been raised with money and around powerful and influential people. He was tall and very handsome, and it was easy to imagine him one day being a successful politician just like his father.

Mike Flannery, on the other hand, was common country stock. Average size, average looks, and probably had never had more than twenty dollars in his pocket at one time. But Deputy Flannery had proven himself to be an outstanding deputy and a credit to the department.

Billy hoped that some of Deputy Flannery's toughness and street savvy would rub off on their new born-of-privilege deputy. It had better, or the mayor's only son, handsome and self-assured Henry Plummer, would not last long in this dangerous and even deadly business.

A clerk popped his head into Billy's office. "Sorry to bother you, but Sheriff Lanier sent a message over that he'd like to see you again and right away."

It only took a second for Billy to form his response. "Tell Sheriff Lanier that if he is in such a red-hot hurry to meet me, then he should deliver his fat ass over here to *my* office."

The clerk's jaw dropped and he gulped before saying, "Do you really want me to tell him those exact words, sir?"

"Yeah, except leave out the 'fat ass' part."

The clerk's face showed his relief. "Yes, sir!"

When the man ducked out of sight, Billy grumbled, "Even if he *does* have a big fat ass."

Chapter 5

The Flannery house was very, very small, and the furnishings were, to be kind, extremely modest and looked to be secondhand.

"Delia, I want you to meet our newest deputy marshal. Henry Plummer and I are going to be working together."

Henry Plummer tried not to gape at the smiling young woman. She was beautiful, with long, shiny black hair, dark brown eyes, and a gorgeous complexion. Delia was almost as tall as her husband and quite voluptuous. Henry thought she might be Italian, or perhaps Greek, but whatever mixes her ancestry was, it had produced a striking beauty.

He bowed slightly. "Very honored to meet you, Mrs. Flannery."

"Call me Delia, please." She turned and beckoned him farther into their home, which, though it was humble, she had decorated with very good taste. "Can I get you some refreshments?"

"No, thank you."

"Then please sit and we'll all get acquainted," Delia said, motioning him toward a sofa. "This is actually the first time that Michael has brought one of his friends from the office to visit."

"I can only stay for a few minutes," Henry told her, although he actually had nothing at all to do the rest of the afternoon.

"Well," Delia said when they were settled in her tiny parlor. "How long have you worked for Marshal Vail and with my husband?"

Henry didn't bother to hide a grin. "Oh," he said, gazing for a moment up at the cracked ceiling, "I'd say about two days."

Delia laughed. "That's not very long." She looked to her husband. "I remember when you started your job and how nervous you were about making a good impression. Hard to believe that you've worked as a federal law officer for almost a year."

"Yeah," Mike Flannery agreed, seeming to enjoy the exchange between Henry and his wife. "Hard to believe."

"Will you two be doing something interesting together, or will you get stuck shuffling papers for a while?"

Henry glanced at his newfound friend then back to the man's wife. He was not sure how much he should tell her and decided that it would be best to let her husband answer that troubling question.

"Well," Michael said. "We're going to be doing some very important work in the next week or two.

And I have tell you that I won't be bathing or shaving until this job is finished. And it would be best if you did the same, Henry."

Delia gave her husband a tepid smile and said, "Why on earth would you and your new friend *not* shave or bathe?"

"We, uh . . . have to sort of get to know some bad sorts so that we can put them behind bars."

Delia could not hide her sudden alarm. "That sounds pretty dangerous! Will you be working closely with my husband, Deputy Plummer?"

"Yes, and we'll both be supervised by Deputy Marshal Custis Long."

"Well, that at least makes me feel a little better," she said with relief. "I've met Marshal Long a couple of times, and we all know of his sterling and outstanding reputation. But still, how dangerous will this new job be?"

Mike Flannery shrugged. "It comes with the territory, Delia. We've talked about this many times. "I know," she argued, "but I never thought that you'd be asked to go amongst evil people and pretend that you are one of them. What would they do if they found out who you *really* are?"

Henry Plummer could see his companion was struggling to find a reassuring answer, but as the seconds ticked by it was obvious that his silence was really upsetting to his new wife. Finally, Henry blurted, "Mrs. Flannery, I mean Delia, I'm sure that your husband will be just fine. Marshal Billy Vail picked your husband over all the others in the office for this *special* assignment."

Delia bit her knuckle for a moment and then forced a smile. "Well, that certainly is a high honor, I suppose." She reached out and took her husband's hand. "I always knew that Michael would do very well as a federal law officer. He is so brave and smart. It's the only job that he's ever wanted. Is it the same way with you, Henry?"

He could not lie to this woman. "In a way, yes. I mean, I wasn't sure if this was exactly the job for me, but I was interested in law enforcement in general, and I'm pretty excited and optimistic about this new career."

"You might as well learn the whole story," Mike Flannery said. "Henry here is almost like royalty. His father is James Flannery, our mayor."

"Well, well! Isn't that something to be proud about!" Delia exclaimed. "How wonderful."

"Thank you," Henry replied. "But being the son of the mayor isn't always an easy thing. I've always been held to an extremely high standard, and my childhood was extremely confining and structured. I went to private schools, studied constantly, and didn't have nearly the fun and boyish adventures that I craved."

"No, I suppose you wouldn't have," Delia said. "And what did your father say when you decided to go to work for the federal marshal's office?"

"He was . . . was neither thrilled nor pleased."

"That must have been a difficult discussion you had with your father."

"It wasn't easy. My father made it very clear years ago that he wanted me to go into banking, real estate, or to become a lawyer. But those professions seem so . . . so bloodless and boring. I may eventually go into law or business, but I couldn't see myself doing that until I reach middle age."

"You were right to stand by your own dreams and to do what your heart says you should," Delia told him.

"True," Henry agreed.

"I want to be a *writer*," Delia announced.

"Is that right?"

"Yes. I've always written stories and I most love writing them for children. I have written at least twenty stories, and some of them have even been printed by small presses back in the East."

"I would love to read a few of them someday."

"Well," Delia said, "I think you would not be impressed by reading little children's stories. And I am constantly improving. Perhaps one day I'll show you a story or two."

"I'll look forward to the day," Henry said, getting up. "Now I'd better go."

Delia frowned with disappointment. "Can't you stay for supper? I have a pot roast that will be ready in about any hour, and I'm sure that you might enjoy a little glass of whiskey or wine."

"Thank you but no," Henry said with more firmness than he felt. "I have made other plans and really need to be leaving. But it was a sincere pleasure meeting you, Delia."

"Don't forget to wear some really bad clothes tomorrow when we meet at the office," Mike Flannery reminded him. "Rub them around in your father's gardens a bit. Don't shave, and try to look dissipated."

"That will be something new," Henry called as he headed for the sidewalk.

"And be well armed!"

Henry decided that he had better see about buying a revolver that very afternoon and remembered how unimpressed Custis Long had been about his sole weapon being a derringer.

"Good-bye, Henry!" Delia called. "Come back soon!"

"I will," he promised, feeling his heart jump in his chest and his breath come a little quicker. He just *had* to get away from the Flannery house before he made a complete fool out of himself and started having indecent thoughts about this stunningly beautiful married woman.

After walking a block back toward town, Henry Plummer actually had no plans at all other than finding ragged clothes and a serviceable pistol. He lived with his father in a very large mansion not far from the Capitol Building. It was a street where big houses sat back far from the street, with imposing lawns tended to by hired gardeners who specialized in rose gardens. It was a house that had servants and cooks, and one that would have completely swallowed up Delia Flannery's modest little bungalow in just a few of its huge rooms.

But Henry wasn't thinking about any of those things. He was thinking that it would someday be nearly miraculous to find as beautiful, charming, intelligent, and mesmerizing a woman as Delia Flannery. And frankly, although he absolutely loathed and was ashamed of himself for thinking it, he could simply not imagine why she had married a very common and not good-looking lawman who was probably making little more than Henry's father's manservant.

Henry was so engrossed in this mystery that he stepped on an ice patch, and the next thing he knew he was sprawled out on the sidewalk.

Serves you right for lusting after another man's wife, he thought, getting up and looking to see if anyone had seen him take his awkward and ungainly spill. Serves you very right indeed, Deputy Henry Plummer.

Chapter 6

"All right," Longarm said the next day, "we've learned that this Hammer Head Saloon is where the Shamrock Gang members hang out from noon usually until after midnight. I've been thinking about this, and it seems pretty unlikely that Henry or you will be noticed by the kind of hard cases that will be coming and going from this place. Unfortunately, I probably *would* be recognized, so I'll have to stay hidden outside and freeze."

Mike Flannery pulled the collar of his dirty coat up around his face. "Sure turned out to be a dark and miserable day. I don't envy you having to wait outside in this cold here while we're inside where it's warm and there's beer."

"Go easy on the beer and avoid the whiskey entirely," Longarm ordered. "The very last thing either of you need is to have too much to drink. I've given you the description of Bully O'Brien, and you shouldn't have any trouble recognizing him. Whoever else is around him you can assume is part of the Shamrock Gang."

"I get that," Henry Plummer said. "But what I don't get is how we're supposed to get friendly with those kinds of low-life criminals."

"I can't give you an answer," Longarm confessed. "What I do know is that you have to let them approach you, not the other way around."

"Easier said than done," Flannery said drily.

"You boys are smart and resourceful, so I've no doubt you'll figure out something. But have a story ready to tell them and then stick to that story. Let them know that you hate the law and there is a reward on your heads. Have names and a little made-up background and make it sound convincing. Throw some money around."

"And where is that money supposed to come from, given the lousy salary we are paid?" Flannery asked.

"Here," Longarm said, handing them each twenty dollars. "I'll get it back from the office fund. You might want to casually drop the word that you have robbed a bank or two in . . . oh, say Utah or Nevada. Being that the Shamrock Gang is just getting into robbing banks, that would draw their interest and attention. They'd want to hear how you did it and maybe pick up some helpful advice."

Deputy Flannery wiped his nose on his sleeve. "I'm ready."

"So am I," Henry Plummer said.

"One last thing," Longarm added before they headed up the street in the lightly falling snow. "If either of you has any sense that they are on to your game, then get out! Don't even think about trying to arrest Bully or his boys. Just come out and meet me right here. Is that understood?"

"But what if we get the drop on them?" Plummer asked. "What if just Bully and maybe one other show up and we can easily arrest them?"

"Don't."

"But . . ."

Longarm grabbed Henry Plummer by the arm and spun him roughly around. "Do exactly as I say. I know it would be quite a feather in your caps to make the arrests, and I am not trying to rob you of that prize . . . but you both lack the experience and you're up against hard and deadly men."

"All right," Henry said. "If they take us for the law, then we'll make a hasty retreat out of the saloon and come running to you like a couple of scared kids."

Longarm didn't like that response, but he let it pass. "Just . . . just stay sober and smart and you'll be fine. Henry, you did buy a pistol and you do know how to use it, right?"

Henry Plummer patted the gun tucked behind his belt. "Of course."

"Good luck."

Longarm watched the two deputies head off into the blowing snow. He was far more nervous about sending green deputies into a lion's den than he would have been if he'd gone in all by himself. But the chance of someone recognizing him in that saloon was too great to take that risk.

An hour passed while Longarm paced back and forth in the snow. He pulled his railroad pocket watch out every fifteen minutes and watched the door of the Hammer Head Saloon as if he were a sinner pining outside the gates of heaven.

Men kept drifting into the saloon, and finally Longarm spotted three that could easily be Bully O'Brien and a couple of his henchmen. Longarm's nerves became tighter than piano wire and he paced faster. An hour dragged past, and he began to wonder whether if he turned up his coat collar and kept his face down, he might be able to enter the seedy saloon and go unnoticed.

No, he decided, as much as I want to be in there in case something goes terribly wrong, I'd be putting their lives at even greater risk by entering the Hammer Head.

Even so, as the cold hours slowly dragged by, Longarm would have given almost anything to be inside that saloon and see how his men were handling the situation and what was actually going on.

"So," the bartender said, pocketing a generous tip and wanting even more, "you boys are new to Denver and are kind of on the run."

"Didn't say that . . . exactly," Henry Plummer said quickly. "But we're keeping our heads down and our guns loaded. Could be some Pinkerton man on our tail, but more likely some asshole from New Mexico."

"Always smart to keep a tight lid on things like that," the bartender agreed, looking around as if he were a close conspirator. "But I get the impression you boys have done pretty well for yourselves riding the outlaw trail."

Mike Flannery pushed out his chest a little and raised his voice so that the Shamrock Gang members would be sure to overhear what he was saying. "Well, we have done pretty damned well for ourselves. My feeling is that some fellas are pickpockets and some are no more than petty thieves . . . but the man who goes after the *big* money is the one to be admired and respected."

Plummer had earlier agreed to play the more modest of the pair. "Now, Henry," he cautioned, "even you have to admit that we were pretty lucky down in Santa Fe last month. That bank was . . . well, never mind."

"You robbed a bank in Santa Fe?" a big man who smelled like a week-old dead horse asked, sliding up next to Henry Plummer. His voice took on an edge. "Or are you boys just blowing a cloud of horseshit over the rest of us?"

Deputy Henry Plummer looked up at Bully O'Brien and smiled. "Mister, me and my partner didn't buy that last round of drinks on the house with horseshit, now did we?"

The bartender laughed. "Hell no you didn't! And to my way of thinking, I'd like to see you men come back any old time you please."

"Well thank you," Henry said. He looked to his friend. "Might be we should be going to get something to eat, huh?"

"Yeah," Mike Flannery agreed. "Drink too much on an empty belly and your brain starts to fuzz up."

"Now, wait a minute," Bully O'Brien objected, laying a heavy hand on both of their shoulders. "You boys have bought everyone here not just one, but *two* rounds. So I'd take it as an insult if you wouldn't allow me to repay you that favor."

Plummer took a moment, as if he were really reflecting on the offer. "All right, we're up for another round and thank you kindly, sir."

"Name is Bully," the man said, sticking out a ham-sized hand. "Bully O'Brien, and these are my friends O'Toole and Hannigan. We're Irishmen to the bone, and you boys look like you might be brothers of the ol' shamrock and sod."

"Well, I am," Flannery said, sporting a wide grin. "But my friend here is a damned Welshman."

Bully O'Brien signaled the bartender to bring them fresh glasses of whiskey. He surveyed his new acquaintances for a minute, and when the drinks had been refreshed, he crowed, "Here's to old men, and to bold men, who take what they please and please no man who tries to shackle them to a steady wage!"

"Or a *prison* cell!" Plummer added.

"That's the spirit!" Bully bellowed, tossing down his drink. "To us brave bastards who plunder till we're six feet under!"

Everyone burst into laughter and more drinks were poured. Bully tossed down two more drinks and then lowered his voice to say, "Why don't you men join us at the table over yonder and we can talk about things that will make us some fresh *money*."

"We never turn away the chance to make money, long as we don't have to work for it," Flannery confided.

"Boys," Bully said, "you are men after my own heart. Bartender, bring us a couple of bottles! They're buyin' one on them, and the other is on Bully and his Shamrock boys."

"Yes, sir."

When the bottles were delivered, Henry paid for one but noticed that Bully O'Brien didn't pay for the other.

"Now," Bully said, leaning across the table, "tell us about that Santa Fe job and how you pulled it off. I'd always heard that Santa Fe has soft and willin' women but is a hard town to rob a bank in."

"Whoever told you that," Flannery replied, "is full of horseshit."

"Ha!" Bully cried, grabbing a bottle and pouring. "We are goin' to have a good time, and I think maybe we can all make this little get-together very profitable."

"How's that?" Plummer asked, as if he hadn't a clue where Bully was going with the conversation.

"You boys seem to know a lot about robbing banks, while me and my boys know the layout of this town. Know every place to get money and every place to hide it. If we put our heads together could be we'll make a fine, lawbreaking team and ride off rich as kings in a few weeks."

"Might be we could at that," Flannery said, trying to look like he'd just been passed a gift of great promise.

"Now," Bully asked, his face eager with anticipation,

"how many banks have you boys actually robbed and how much cash have you gotten away with this past year?"

Flannery's phony smile faded. He and Plummer had come up with a plausible story but had not thought to come up with actual figures. "Well . . ."

"Come on, boys! This is not the time to be bashful about your accomplishments," Bad Barry Hennigan urged. "Give us the straight story."

Mick O'Toole nodded. "If we're going to be partners, you got to come straight with us."

"Fair enough," Flannery finally agreed. "Right?"

Henry Plummer nodded, looking very serious. "Yeah, that makes sense."

"All right then," Bully said. "Let's get down to some real serious talk and see if we can come to a meeting of criminal minds."

The Shamrock Gang members knew that Bully was making a joke and laughed, but it was all that Henry Plummer and Mike Flannery could do just to dredge up an agreeable smile.

"Got a bank in mind?" Plummer asked.

"Any bank that has a bundle ought to do," Bully said.

"It's more complicated than that," Plummer said.

"We didn't think so when we robbed a couple. No problems."

"Then you were lucky," Flannery told them. "Did these banks have any armed guards?"

"No," Bully admitted. "They were real small banks."

"And how much cash did you get?"

Bully took a drink. "Not too much, but . . ."

"If we're going to rob a bank," Flannery whispered, eyes going to each man at the table, "we're going to rob a big, prosperous bank."

"Higher risk," Bully pointed out, looking a little worried.

"Higher risk means higher reward," Plummer said.

Bully's eyes were bloodshot but intense. "How much money are we talking about?"

"Over ten thousand or it's not worth the risk."

"Ten thousand!"

"That's half of what we got in Santa Fe."

"Did you boys kill any guards that day?" Hannigan wanted to know.

"Only one," Flannery said as if it were nothing. "We did real good that day."

The Shamrock Gang exchanged glances, and then Bully said, "We haven't had to kill anyone yet . . . but we'll do what is needed providing the money is there."

"That's the part we specialize in," Flannery said.

"How?"

Flannery smiled. "We set up a phony account and check out the bank real good. We put some planning into it, so that when we walk in the door with guns in our hands, we know that we're not just gonna walk out with pocket money."

"That's right," Plummer said. "Big risks . . . big rewards."

"We're in with you," Bully O'Brien said, sticking out his great paw. "Right, boys?"

All of them nodded, and as they poured fresh glasses and made a toast to a new and successful partnership, Henry Plummer could feel a cold, nervous sweat trickle down from his armpits.

Chapter 7

It was just after midnight when Longarm saw his two young deputies stagger out of the Hammer Head Saloon, and by then he was so damned cold he could have pissed yellow icicles.

And he was mad, real mad.

He watched deputies Flannery and Plummer boisterously laugh and shake hands with Bully O'Brien and his Shamrock Gang thieves and thugs.

They drank too damn much, Longarm thought to himself. They used that government expense account money to have themselves a high old time, and by damned they'd better have something important to tell me or I'll wring both their necks!

The two groups parted ways, and Longarm remained well in the shadows until his deputies were almost past him. Then, stepping out and grabbing both young men by the collar, he whirled them around.

"What the hell were you doing in there so long!"

Both Henry Plummer and Mike Flannery tried to speak at the same time, and when that didn't work, they plastered stupid grins on their faces.

"Come on," Longarm said, shoving both men up the street. "We're going to get some food and coffee in you, and then I'm going to decide whether or not I should ask Billy Vail to pull your badges for good."

"He'd do that?" Flannery asked.

"Hell yes he would," Longarm snapped.

An hour later Longarm sat across the table from them in a small all-night diner and listened to what his deputies had to say for themselves.

"We're going to rob a bank," Flannery said.

"Who is 'we'?" Longarm demanded.

"Us and Bully O'Brien and his Shamrock Gang."

"When?"

"Tomorrow," Plummer said.

"No," his partner said. "*Today*."

Longarm leaned forward. "You are going to go with them and hit a bank today?"

"That's right," Flannery said. "We agreed to meet with Bully and his men at three o'clock this afternoon, and plan to go directly to the Bank of Denver's South End branch down on South Federal."

"I know the bank," Longarm said. "They were robbed two years ago, and the bank manager was able to grab a shotgun, which cost him his life and that of a customer."

"Bully didn't say anything about that," Flannery replied.

Longarm thought for a moment. "How many men do you think Bully O'Brien will have on this job?"

"I don't know because he never said. Maybe just the pair he had with him tonight."

"We should expect more," Longarm told them.

Henry Plummer rubbed his face. "I need to sober up and get some sleep."

"Me, too," Flannery agreed. "Custis, can you . . ."

"Yeah," Longarm agreed. "I'll go tell our boss what the plan is, and he and I can decide who needs to be waiting and how we'll handle this. Most important thing is that no innocent bystanders get shot in a cross fire."

Longarm glanced up at the clock in Marshal Billy Vail's office. "They're going into that bank in two hours. I think I need to get moving so I'll have time to get in a good firing position outside."

"Deputy Hugh Reed and Deputy Joe Hector will give us enough backup if they're needed," Billy said. "I'm coming along as well."

"I'm not sure that's such a good idea," Longarm told his boss.

"And why not? Do you think I'll botch things up because I've been sitting behind this desk too long?"

"I didn't say that."

"You didn't need to." Billy hadn't been in the field for almost two years, and Longarm doubted if he'd fired his gun in all that time. "I'll pretend to be one of the bank's customers when they come in to hold it up. Deputy Reed can be acting like another customer, and Deputy Hector can be outside waiting near you. We'll need to clear out the real customers before the Shamrock Gang comes through the bank's front door."

"It won't work," Longarm said. "If they arrive a little early to check out the bank and see that there are only two customers inside and that they are both armed men, then the gang might get spooked. I think it might be best if you stay here. I'll report back"

"If we can take Bully O'Brien and his men alive, that would be best. But if not . . ."

"I know," Longarm said. "After the gang goes inside, I'll move toward the front door of the bank but keep a distance. We'll also have to worry about Deputy Flannery and Deputy Plummer. Especially Plummer, who admits that he's a poor shot."

"I wish that he wasn't going to be in there," Billy muttered. "If something goes wrong and he's killed . . . or even wounded . . . his father is going to raise hell."

"What can the mayor do to you?" Longarm asked as they were leaving. "I understand that he could fire anyone under him, but we're feds."

"It all ties together," Billy said. "Trust me, Mayor Plummer is a good man, but I know that Henry is his only son and if this whole thing goes awry, heads will roll . . . and maybe they'll be ours."

"Right now," Longarm said, turning to leave. "City politics is the very last thing on my mind."

"There they are," Joe Hector said, sliding back out of sight near Longarm. "There are *six* of them!"

"Just make damn sure you know which ones are our deputies."

"I couldn't miss Plummer given how tall he is, and I recognize Flannery by his walk."

"Yeah, me too."

Longarm watched as five men went into the bank, leaving a sixth outside the entrance as a watchman. "Damn, I didn't think they'd be smart enough to post a lookout!"

"What are we going to do about him?" Hector asked.

Longarm's mind was racing. He knew that he had less than a minute before all hell was going to break loose inside the bank. "I'm going to try and take him without him giving his friends inside any warning. Just move in closer but not too close to me, Joe."

"I got a bad feeling in my gut about this," Joe Hector said as they moved forward. "This just doesn't feel right."

"Shut up and stay back! If that lookout sees us both coming toward him, he's probably going to panic."

Longarm kept his head down and walked as fast as he dared without attracting too much attention. He moved across the street, and as he neared the bank the lookout began to watch him closely while moving his hand to the butt of his holstered pistol.

"Hey," the man said, "you goin' into the bank?"

"Yeah. I was planning to," Longarm replied. "Why do you ask?"

"Uh . . . the bank is closed. The office manager died, I think."

Longarm paused in mid-stride, but then he kept coming.

"Hey, I said—"

The lookout's words were cut short by the sound of gunfire inside the bank. Longarm saw the lookout's hand move toward his own gun, and that's when Longarm threw a straight right cross that hit the man directly in the nose, causing it to break and gush blood. Longarm slammed an uppercut to the lookout's stomach and shoved him aside as he took the bank's stairs two at a time. There was so much gunfire inside the bank that it sounded like a war.

Longarm threw open the door with his gun coming up in his hand. He saw gunsmoke and men firing at one another at close range. Some were down; some were bent over and obviously critically wounded, but still firing.

It was every lawman's worst nightmare.

Chapter 8

Longarm hesitated, eyes blinking rapidly as he stood framed in the doorway trying to make sure that he correctly identified Flannery and Plummer. But there was a wild card to consider . . . What if one of the men shooting was a bank employee?

Suddenly, Bully O'Brien emerged from the cloud of gunsmoke, staggering toward Longarm and the door. He was looking back over his shoulder and still firing when Longarm shot him through the back of the head. O'Brien crashed into the doorway and Longarm jumped over his body, yelling, "Flannery! Plummer, it's Custis!"

There was a flurry of final gunshots, and then only two men were standing, Henry Plummer and Longarm, who jumped over another body and knelt beside Deputy Mike Flannery.

"Mike!"

Longarm shook the man, but from the rapidly spreading pool of blood underneath him it was clear that Flannery had died in the furious gun battle. "Oh, damn!" Longarm whispered just as Henry Plummer collapsed to the floor, gun spilling from his hand.

Longarm had started to move toward Plummer, when a Shamrock Gang member raised his head, aimed his pistol, and fired. The bullet clipped Longarm's gunbelt and splintered its way through a desk. Longarm spun away from Deputy Plummer and shot the man twice, just to make sure there would be no more surprises.

"Henry, how badly are you hit!"

"Help!" someone yelled from behind the teller's cage. "I'm shot and need a doctor!"

Suddenly, there were other cries pleading for help. A woman began to sob somewhere in the bank, and Henry Plummer whispered, trying to smile with a bad joke, "I'm sure glad I didn't go into banking."

Longarm yelled for Joe Hector to run for a doctor. He made a hurried examination of his young deputy and determined that Plummer had been shot at least twice in the body and once in the thigh. However, none of the body wounds seemed to be dead center, and both might have missed any vital organs.

"Just hang on, Henry. We're getting a doctor here as soon as we can."

"I missed with my first two shots, but I killed Mick O'Toole before I went down." Plummer grimaced and whispered, "How . . . how is Deputy Flannery?"

"He didn't make it," Longarm answered in a voice that even he didn't recognize.

Henry Plummer began to weep and rage. "Dammit, Custis, this didn't go *anything* like I expected."

"It rarely does."

"Mike Flannery saved my life. He jumped in between me and Bully and took a bullet that I should have taken. Then he—"

Longarm put a hand over the badly wounded deputy's mouth. "You can tell us all what went wrong later. Right now I've got to see if I can help anyone else." He pulled a handkerchief out of his coat pocket. "Henry, you're bleeding pretty badly from the bullet you took in your upper right leg. Can you press this down on it to slow the bleeding?"

"Sure. Go see what you can do for the others. There were two women in the bank, and I managed to shove one behind a desk, but she was so scared that I'm not sure that she made it. She might have jumped up in panic and gotten herself killed."

"I'll find out," Longarm promised. "Just hold this handkerchief down tight on that leg. I'll be back soon."

The gunsmoke was clearing and Longarm quickly took an accounting. A woman caught in the cross fire, with cash still clutched in her hand, was dead because a bullet to the neck had severed an artery. Another woman, probably the one that Henry Plummer had saved by shoving her behind cover, was hysterical but unscathed. Three bank employees at the back of the room were hiding under their desks, faces pale and wearing terrified expressions. The manager of the bank was unconscious, shot all to hell and dying.

Longarm calmed the young woman and pulled her out from under her desk. "It's over," he said. "It's over and you're going to be all right."

She was pretty and plump. With a huge sob she

threw her arms around Longarm in a death-like grip and would not let him go until he pried her fingers apart and then led her outside over Bully O'Brien's body and that of another member of the Shamrock Gang.

Moments later, Deputy Hector burst inside dragging a young doctor.

"Jaysus!" the doctor whispered. "This place looks like a slaughterhouse!"

"Take care of that deputy before he bleeds to death," Longarm ordered. "The bank manager is over there in the corner, but I'm pretty sure that he's not going to make it."

"What a bloodbath," the doctor breathed as he hurried over to attend to Deputy Plummer. "I don't care how much damn money they would have taken . . . better that than all these people dying!"

Longarm didn't have a response or the will to argue the point. Instead, he went outside, followed by Deputy Joe Hector. The lookout that Longarm had knocked senseless had been shot dead on the front steps. Maybe by Hector but perhaps he had blundered back inside and taken a random bullet.

"Custis, what do you think went so wrong?"

"I don't know yet," Longarm admitted. "The plan was that deputies Flannery and Plummer were going to let the gang take the money without incident and wait until they were out on the street. With Flannery and Plummer behind Bully and his boys and with me and you in front of the gang, we'd have had them boxed from both sides and in a cross fire. We thought they'd surrender rather than die."

"But . . ."

Longarm shook his head and his voice was bitter. "Something went wrong *inside* the bank and our plan never had a chance. We'll find out what happened when Deputy Plummer is able to talk."

"You think he'll survive?"

"He was shot three times, but I don't think any of his wounds are fatal," Longarm said. "Now, don't ask me any more questions, Joe. Just . . . just go back into the bank and see what you can do to calm people down and get them out of there."

"All right," Hector said. "What are you going to do now?"

Longarm wanted a few shots of whiskey, but he had things to do first. "I'm going to find Marshal Vail and give him a sketchy report of what went wrong."

"There will be hell to pay from the mayor's office. And if Henry doesn't make it . . ."

"I know," Longarm said. "But we can't worry about that right now. I have a woman to tell that she's just become a widow."

"Mrs. Flannery."

"Yes," Longarm said. "And it's a job that I dread more than anything in this world."

"If you want," Hector offered, "I'll go tell Delia that her husband is dead."

"Do you know Mrs. Flannery?"

"Yeah. I know her a little."

Longarm was more than tempted to let his deputy do the sad job of informing the new widow what had happened to her husband inside the bank, but that would have been shirking his duty, and he had never in his life ducked something just because it was hard to do.

"Thanks, Joe, but I'll tell her."

"She's going to take it real hard. She and Mike were really a fine match. They loved each other so much."

"Yeah," Longarm said, his mind still whirling from all the death and all the terrible things he'd just witnessed. "I'm sure she did. Deputy Mike Flannery was an outstanding officer and a good man to stand with in a fight."

"I really admired him," Hector said, voice thick with emotion. "Mike was always so dedicated to duty. Just like you, Custis."

Longarm had no response. With the sounds of gunfire still booming inside his head, along with the image of blood splatters on the wall and pools of it on the bank's polished hardwood floor, he walked away feeling half-sick and awful.

"It was me that shot the lookout," Hector called down the street. "He was getting up with a gun in his fist and . . ."

Longarm didn't hear the rest of that story. At the moment, he was consumed by questions and an overwhelming sense of failure.

Why did Billy Vail and I ever think that we should send a newly hired deputy and one without much more than a year of experience into that bank with Bully O'Brien and his Shamrock Gang of cold-blooded killers? he asked himself. And why hadn't they let the gang take the money and come outside just like we planned?

Chapter 9

Longarm knew where Mike Flannery had lived with his wife, and now, with the day going long and two strong shots of whiskey under his belt, he stood outside of their white picket fence with his hand frozen on the gate's latch.

He had often heard from the men in his office that Mike and Delia Flannery had been deeply in love and that the woman was breathtakingly beautiful. But none of that really mattered anymore.

Longarm could not bring himself to open the gate.

Delia stepped out onto her little front porch, and for a moment they both seemed frozen in time. Then, without him saying a word, her hands flew to her face and she let out a deep, sorrowful moan, screaming, "Oh, no!"

Standing beside her latched gate, hearing that sound

and watching her break up wounded Longarm more deeply than any knife blade or bullet ever could.

He unlatched the gate, but she had already whirled and run back inside to shut her front door. Longarm walked up to the porch and sat down on the steps. He'd stay there for an hour or two just in case she decided she needed a shoulder to cry on or a sympathetic ear ready to listen. Longarm knew that Delia would soon be asking questions . . . and they were mostly ones he could not yet answer.

Two hours later and just about the time that the sun was setting in the west, Delia came out with two cups of coffee and quietly sat down beside him. Her eyes were red, her face drawn, and her expression had about it the look of devastation.

"I only have two questions for you right now," she managed to say. "Did my husband die bravely and while trying to carry out his duties?"

"Yes. He saved Henry Plummer's life by pushing him to one side and taking a bullet."

She nodded and wiped at tears. "And did he die . . . quickly or . . ."

"He died very quickly and didn't suffer, ma'am." Longarm swallowed hard. "I . . . I just don't have the words to tell you how liked and respected your husband was by all of us in the federal office."

"Michael loved his job and he wouldn't have considered doing anything else." She gently placed her hand on Longarm's hand, and hers felt very cold. "I knew that Michael and Deputy Plummer were going to do something very dangerous together today.

Michael didn't want to talk about it and neither did Henry. So Henry's alive?"

"Yes." Longarm took a deep breath. "But he is pretty shot up. He's been rushed to the hospital. He was bleeding pretty badly when I got to him in the bank, but none of the wounds appeared to be fatal."

"If he was standing tall beside my husband when the fight began and my husband saved his life, then I need to see him."

"I'm sure that would be welcomed by Henry," Longarm said. "But . . . but you need to wait until we know for certain that he's going to make it."

"If he's going to die, I want to be there before he passes."

Longarm looked into her grief-stricken eyes. "Why?"

She shrugged. "Michael told me that he really liked Henry. Said he was going to make a fine deputy, even though he could have done most anything else because of his father's money and position as our mayor. The fact that he chose to be sworn in as a federal deputy marshal in that office really meant something to my husband. I'd like to tell Deputy Plummer that to his face, so that he knows that my husband died beside a man he really cared about."

"I understand."

"Then let's go and find where they've taken Henry Plummer."

The sun was just starting to set and the temperature was dropping fast. "Right now?"

"Yes, right now. If Henry has died of his wounds, then I will *still* tell him what I just told you. And if

Henry is alive, he'll want to hear what I have to say so that he isn't filled with guilt because my husband saved his life today."

Longarm pushed himself to his feet and nodded. "All right, Mrs. Flannery, let's go see where they've taken Deputy Plummer . . . to the hospital or the morgue . . . so that we can both pay our respects."

"Thank you, I'll get my coat because it's getting very cold out. It feels like it might even snow tonight."

Longarm waited, and when Delia returned from inside, he offered her his arm and they headed down the street. "Be careful," he cautioned, "it's almost to the freezing point and this street is getting icy and slick."

"Nothing can hurt me more than I'm already hurt."

"We'll just watch our steps," Longarm told her. "Most likely Henry is at the Denver Memorial Hospital. Maybe we can hail a horse-and-buggy driver to—"

"I'd rather walk with you and breathe in some cold, fresh air, if you don't mind."

Longarm didn't mind at all, and he sure did hope that the doctors had gotten Deputy Henry Plummer's wounds to stop bleeding. If the bullets to his body had pierced organs, Henry was almost assuredly dead. But if not, he seemed likely to survive.

Longarm wanted to walk faster, but with Delia on his right arm and the ice starting to crunch beneath his feet, he needed to walk slow and easy.

It had been a nightmare of a day, and he'd be going to hell if he let either himself or the beautiful widow on his arm fall.

Chapter 10

"Doctor, is Deputy Henry Plummer still alive or . . ."

The doctor looked at Longarm and then at the woman on his arm. "And you are . . . ?"

"We're friends," Longarm said. "Deputy Plummer works with me, and this lady is Mrs. Flannery. Her husband was gunned down in that attempted bank robbery where Deputy Plummer was badly wounded."

"I see." The doctor looked exhausted. He wiped a hand across his face and took a deep breath. "Well, the good news is that Deputy Plummer is going to live. But the bad news is that he has lost a lot of blood, and while the two wounds to his body missed organs, the bullet to his leg shattered the thigh bone."

Longarm swallowed hard. "Are you going to have to amputate?"

"We're not sure."

"What does that mean?" Longarm demanded.

"It means what I just said . . . we're not sure. Given

how much blood Deputy Plummer has already lost, in my professional opinion, amputation would cause even more blood loss and he'd almost certainly go into severe shock and die."

"Then *don't* amputate."

The doctor was in his fifties and heavyset, with large dark circles under his eyes. He ran his fingers through his thin, straw-colored hair and said, "Mayor Plummer just arrived and is with his son, who remains unconscious. His vital signs are weak and things are touch-and-go. If we don't operate now, sepsis might set into the thigh bone, and a bone infection could take the young man's life."

"So," Delia said, "if you operate, he's almost sure to die of shock, and if you don't operate, he may die of infection?"

"I'm afraid that's about the size of it," the doctor replied. "I gave the head of the hospital and my superior my medical opinion. Now they're passing that information on to Mayor Plummer, who, as the young man's only living relative, will decide what should be done for his son."

Longarm nodded. "I see."

"The decision is not ours to make," the doctor said. "And Mrs. Flannery, may I extend my sincerest condolences for the loss of your brave husband today. I had heard that several people died in the bank, including a federal officer. I am very sorry."

"Thank you."

"Would you both like to come back tomorrow . . . or perhaps take a seat in our hospital's waiting room? I'm not sure if Mayor Plummer will be staying the night or leaving. However, I am quite sure that he will not allow anyone to visit his son. He is extremely upset, as you can well understand."

"Of course," Delia said. "We are all devastated by what happened at the bank."

"Marshal," the doctor dared to say, "for the very life of me I cannot understand why a shoot-out was allowed to occur *inside* the bank when there were employees and customers all around."

"It wasn't supposed to happen like that," Longarm said quietly. "Something unexpected went wrong inside the bank."

"It sounds to me like *everything* went wrong." The doctor glanced over his shoulder and down the hall. "I feel that I need to warn you, Marshal Long, that the mayor is enraged concerning what happened. Given that warning, my advice would be for you and Mrs. Flannery to avoid him until things sort themselves out."

"Meaning," Delia said, "until Deputy Plummer either lives or dies."

"To be blunt, that is exactly my meaning."

"Thank you, Doctor." Longarm took Delia's arm and led her down the hallway into the waiting room. "I feel as if I need to stay until Henry either makes it or doesn't. However, there are cabdrivers that regularly come up to the front drive, and I will hail one and he will take you home."

"No," she said. "What would I do there all alone? Go to pieces?" She took Longarm's hand and squeezed it hard. "If I remain right here and pray very hard about Henry Plummer pulling through this, then that will also help me get through tonight."

"I understand," Longarm said, taking a seat beside her. He was about to say more, but just at that moment, Billy Vail hurried inside the hospital. When he spotted Longarm and Delia, he changed direction.

"Mrs. Flannery, I am so very sorry about what happened."

"I know."

"My office is at your disposal, and we will do whatever we can to help you through this time of great sorrow. All of us at the Federal Building had the highest regard for Deputy Flannery."

"Thank you."

Billy looked to Longarm, and it was clear that he struggled to ask the question that was foremost on his mind. "How is Deputy Plummer?"

Longarm gave him the news they had just received, and Billy's face turned ashen. "So we're just waiting to see what will happen?"

"That's right," Longarm said. "I offered to help Mrs. Flannery get back to her house, but she wants to stay here until Henry either makes it . . . or doesn't."

Billy Vail sat down beside them and bent his head low. "I just don't know what could have gone wrong in the bank. I just can't understand what might have happened in there to make things turn out the way that they did."

"You want to hear my guess?" Longarm asked quietly.

"Sure."

"I'm guessing that when Bully O'Brien and his boys pulled their guns, one of them shot someone. Maybe a clerk or the bank manager. Either that or someone in the bank, a depositor or an employee, foolishly pulled a weapon, and then it was a close-quartered gunfight with very few survivors."

"That's what I was thinking on the way over here. We'll interview everyone that was inside the bank this afternoon and get some answers. I have been over at the bank, and Deputy Hector has gotten everyone's name and address. We'll find out what happened and make sure it never happens again."

"Yeah," Longarm said, "but it's all a little late now."

Two hours later they were still sitting anxiously in the waiting room when the familiar figure of Mayor James Flannery emerged around a corner in the hallway. The mayor looked shaken to his core and did not even see the trio waiting to hear news about his son until he was nearly past them.

"Mayor," Billy Vail said, "how is your son?"

Mayor Flannery seemed to snap out of a bad dream, and it took him a split second to focus and then recognize Marshal Vail. When he did, his face darkened with anger and he hissed, "You! You're the one that is responsible for that slaughter that took place in the bank today! And for the loss of innocent people's lives! How in God's name could you have sent two *inexperienced* deputies into that bank!"

Billy was so shaken by the man's fury that he couldn't speak for a moment. Delia, however, stood up and said, "My husband, Deputy Mike Flannery, died today in that bank, and he was *not* inexperienced, Mayor Plummer."

Longarm had been about to jump up and restrain

the mayor, who looked angry enough to attack Billy Vail. Now, however, Delia Flannery's sudden and unexpected defense of her late husband had defused an explosive confrontation.

"Miss Flannery, I . . . I am sorry. I didn't mean to insult your brave husband or in any way tarnish his good name or character. It's just that my son is . . ."

Mayor Flannery, a man known for his courage and honor, suddenly broke down in front of them. He covered his face and began to sob uncontrollably. Delia hugged him and then they both cried.

Longarm couldn't bear it anymore. He headed for the exit of the hospital, and for the next several hours all he did was walk and think, and with each stride he resolved that he would somehow make restitution for everything that had gone wrong this day.

Starting with doing what he was best at . . . finding criminals. The ones that he most wanted to find now were the pair of brothers formerly named Dirk and Harold Raney, who had murdered Mayor Plummer's wife many years ago, forever robbing a six-year-old boy of his young mother.

Yes, Longarm thought, I can't change a thing that happened today, but I can do something to atone. I will track that pair down and either arrest or kill them. Henry said they are in Denver, but I will find them even if they have left town and gone to hell. I will find them because that is the only thing I can do to make amends and exact some long overdue restitution.

Chapter 11

Longarm returned to his office the next morning to find a haggard-looking Billy Vail seated behind his desk just staring at the wall.

"Morning, Billy."

"I don't know what is good about it."

"Have you heard any more about how Deputy Plummer is doing at the hospital?"

"I sent a man over about six o'clock this morning. He came back and told me that Henry is still hanging on and that they've decided not to amputate that leg. I guess they just patched it up after digging out any lead that they could find, and they're hoping that it heals without complications. But one of the doctors said that Henry Plummer will always have a pronounced limp, and that leg could give him a lot of pain over the years."

"Well," Longarm said glumly, "at least he didn't get killed like poor Deputy Flannery."

"Yeah, at least we have that to be thankful for," Billy said without enthusiasm. "Our mayor delivered a message to me."

"I can hardly wait to hear it," Longarm said.

"Mayor Plummer wants a full investigation of what went wrong in that bank. He is bent on trying to get me removed from this office."

"Can he do that?"

Billy shrugged. "I honestly don't know. Mayor Flannery has some powerful connections. He can put my feet to the fire."

"His connections are most likely all right here in Colorado. We're federal officers and . . ."

"Custis, the mayor has friends in Washington, D.C. I don't know if he can get me fired or not, but he is likely to try. He's coming over here as soon as his son's condition stabilizes, and the meeting isn't going to be friendly."

Longarm sat down and scowled. "I can't say that I blame our mayor too much. His son is far too green to have been asked to make friends with the Shamrock Gang and pretend to be a part of that bank robbery. I also think we were pushing it by asking Mike Flannery to take that assignment."

"What choice was there?" Billy asked. "My face is well known and so is yours, and we couldn't risk the chance that Bully O'Brien or one of his men would recognize us. And my other deputies are all working on cases that I couldn't pull them away from."

"So what can I do to take the heat off you?"

"I want you to question anyone who was inside the bank when the robbery and the shooting took place. I had thought that we could just wait and have Deputy Plummer fill us in, but we're running out of time."

Longarm stood up. "I'll go and find out exactly what happened yesterday."

"Do that," Billy urged. "And it sure would help if you could return and give me a report before the mayor arrives."

"Understood," Longarm said.

Twenty minutes later Longarm approached the bank, but it was locked and shuttered. He hammered on the front door, and finally a woman's face appeared behind the window. Longarm showed her his badge and motioned for her to unlock the door. The woman hesitated for a moment and then did as instructed.

The first thing he noticed when he got inside was that someone had already washed and scrubbed the blood off the floor. The furniture that had been overturned had been set right, but there were bullet holes in the walls, desks, and even a few in the ceiling. The air inside had the odor of blood and bleach.

"My name is Deputy Marshal Custis Long. Who are you, ma'am?"

She looked nervous and frightened. Her eyes were red and puffy and she kept wringing her hands. She was a slender, delicate-looking woman in her forties and still quite attractive, but right now she seemed to have trouble focusing her attention on Longarm.

"What is your name?"

"Miss Agnes Peterson. I've worked here for eleven years."

"Doing what?" Longarm asked.

"Clerical work and whatever is asked." Her lower lip began to tremble. "Today even though the bank was closed, I came in all by myself to . . . to clean things up."

He knew she meant the blood.

"I'm sure that the bank has someone else who does the cleaning, Miss Peterson."

"But not the . . . the blood!"

Agnes burst into fresh tears, and Longarm gently led her over to a chair and waited while she regained her composure. When she finally did, he knelt at her side and said, "I am very sorry about what happened. It must have been a nightmare."

"It was *worse* than any nightmare," she whispered, big tears rolling down her pale cheeks. "I saw a lot of people die right here in this room. Mr. Madison tried to shield me from the gunfire, and he died for his bravery."

"Who is he?"

"Our manager. Mr. Madison was very kind. A wonderful, generous man always trying to help others. I've worked for him since the very beginning. We were friends and he trusted me."

"I'm sure that you earned that trust." Longarm pulled up a chair. "Miss Peterson, did you see everything that happened?"

"Most of it. But it all happened so fast that it is hazy in my mind, and I generally have a very good mind."

"Tell me exactly what happened."

"I'm not sure that I can, Marshal."

"Try. It's very important."

Agnes took a deep, shuddering breath. "I was

behind the teller's cages doing my usual accounting work when a bunch of men came into the bank. They didn't yell or use their guns; they just marched straight across the lobby, and then the next thing I knew they were back where we do not allow the public."

"Back here where we are right now."

"That's right. Mr. Madison was standing only a few feet away from me discussing something with one of the tellers when the robbers pulled their guns and demanded that everyone lie down on the floor."

"And did they?"

"Everyone but Mr. Madison. You see, this bank was robbed once before, and so Mr. Madison always carried a little pistol in his coat pocket."

"Probably a derringer," Longarm decided. "Surely he didn't pull that and try to fend off the bank robbers."

"He did, but at the same time he jumped for his office, where he kept a rifle. When he did that, he was shot, and that's when I screamed and tried to run to his side and help him. He cried out something, pulled me down and sort of rolled over on top of me like a shield."

"And then what happened?"

"I heard someone shout, 'No!'"

"One of the robbers."

"Yes. The voice was loud and unfamiliar. The next thing I knew, two of the bank robbers were shooting at some of the others. I . . . I still don't understand what happened. But I was so frightened that I crawled behind a desk and curled up in a little ball. I was sure that everyone in the bank was going to die. When the shooting finally stopped, I could hear people shouting and moaning. I climbed out from under the desk and there was blood *everywhere*. It looked to me like most everyone was either dead or dying."

"And then what . . ." Longarm stopped in mid-sentence because Agnes Peterson's eyes were growing wide and she started to tremble. "I saw you come through the front door and you were shooting . . ."

Suddenly, the woman's eyes rolled up and she fainted.

Longarm eased her down onto the floor, took off his coat, and tucked it in around her. He looked for water and didn't see any, so he took a chair and waited about five minutes until she regained consciousness.

"Is there some water around that I could give you to drink?" he asked.

"Over there in that big crock we keep fresh water. There are some glasses on the counter to the right."

Longarm brought the poor woman a cool glass of water, which she drank down in gulps.

"Miss Peterson, do you think that the bank robbers intended to harm all of you or just rob the bank and leave?"

"There is no doubt in my mind that they were going to murder *all* of us."

"Why do you think that?"

"Because everyone knew who they were . . . or at least we recognized Bully O'Brien and a couple of his men. And I remember one of them saying, 'We can't let them put the finger on us. We have to kill them.'"

"That's *exactly* what you heard one of the men say?"

"Yes, and that's when Mr. Peterson reached for his little gun and tried to defend us."

Longarm thought about that for several moments before he asked, "You said that two of the men who came in with the bank robbers turned on them and began shooting."

"Yes."

"Any idea why they would do that?"

"None whatsoever. All I know is that one minute we were facing our executioners and the next instant everyone was firing and I was leaping for cover."

"Miss Peterson, what you've just told me is very important and helpful."

Agnes expelled a deep breath. "I'm glad to hear that. Who were the two that turned on Bully O'Brien and his Shamrock Gang? And why did they do that?"

"They were United States deputy marshals just like me. They had gained Bully's trust and they were going to let him rob this bank, and when they came outside we were going to arrest the gang on the street."

"But . . ."

"I know," Longarm said. "We never counted on them executing everyone in the bank. And when those young and brave deputies realized that something terrible was going to happen, they had no choice but to draw their guns and open fire at close quarters."

"Did they both die?"

"One of them did, but the other one is still fighting for his life."

"The tall one."

"Yes."

"What is his name?"

"Henry Plummer."

Agnes sniffled. "He and the other deputy had no

choice but to start shooting or let us all die. Marshal, your brave men did what they had to do."

"I'm very glad you said that," Longarm told the woman. "Now, I think we need to leave this place and get you home, because being here alone at the bank is not good for you, Miss Peterson. Not good at all."

"No, it isn't, and I'm so tired. I didn't sleep last night, and I couldn't get the picture of all that death out of my mind. I . . . I don't know if I'll ever recover from what happened here yesterday."

"You will," he assured her. "I have seen a lot of death and know the toll it takes on people. Some survivors never get over the shock and horror, but others mend themselves in time."

"I'm not sure if I can mend."

"I think that you can and will. But right now, Miss Peterson, will you let me escort you home?"

"I would like that."

Longarm helped the fragile woman to her feet and then to the front door, where she paused to whisper, "I don't believe I can ever work here again with Mr. Madison gone."

"Did the man have a family?"

"No. He was a confirmed bachelor. He had his . . . his eccentricities and wasn't always the easiest man to be around, but I understood him well and he was a good person. He was all I ever thought a man should be."

"I'm sure that he was."

She bit her lower lip. "You've probably already guessed that I loved him deeply."

"And I'll bet that he also loved you."

She managed the smallest of smiles. "Yes, he did.

And I believe that, had we been given another year working together, he would have asked me out to dinner, and then we would have kissed, and someday we'd have married."

Longarm didn't know how to respond, so after she locked up the bank, he took Agnes Peterson by the arm and led her away.

Chapter 12

Longarm stepped into Billy Vail's office and came face-to-face with Mayor James Flannery. They had met before in passing, and their interaction had always been cordial, but it wouldn't be that way today.

Billy Vail stood up behind his desk with a grim expression. "Custis, I'm sure you know Mayor Flannery."

"I do." Longarm extended his hand, which was ignored.

Mayor Flannery was an imposing physical specimen of manhood. He was well over six feet tall, and although he was in his mid-fifties, he looked to be strong and fit. His dark brown hair was slicked straight back, and he had a neatly trimmed beard and piercing brown eyes, Longarm could see a lot of Deputy Henry Plummer in his wealthy and successful father.

"I understand," the mayor said, biting his words out

like chips flying off flint, "that you are equally responsible for the disaster at the Bank of Denver yesterday in which eight people died and many, including my son, were critically wounded."

"Yes. We lost Deputy Mike Flannery and the bank manager, in addition to the ones that were going to murder and rob everyone in that bank."

The mayor blinked. "And exactly *how* do you know that Bully O'Brien and his thugs were going to murder innocent bank employees and customers?"

"I interviewed a woman named Miss Agnes Peterson less than an hour ago. I found her alone in the bank after she had scrubbed blood off the bank's floors. She was, as you would expect, extremely shaken and upset, but she could tell me what happened in the bank and why it turned into a bloody gun battle."

The mayor took a deep, steadying breath and glanced at Billy Vail, who said, "I think we should both hear what Miss Peterson had to say to my finest deputy. Mayor, please take a seat and let's see if we can try and understand exactly what did happen in the bank."

The mayor's square jaw was clenched tight, and it took some effort for him to take a seat. When he spoke, his voice shook with fury. "No matter what provoked the gun battle, if you really did know that the Shamrock Gang was going to rob the bank, you should have stopped them *before* they even entered it, gawdammit!"

"We didn't yet have anything to arrest them for," said Billy pointedly.

The mayor turned to Longarm. "Get started, Deputy."

Longarm wasn't accustomed to being talked to in that

manner, but under the circumstances the mayor's attitude was completely understandable and even justified.

"Miss Peterson told me that when the gang, your son Henry, and his fellow deputy Mike Flannery entered the bank, the bank employees' understanding was that it was just going to be a robbery and that no one was to be hurt or killed. But that changed when one of the gang members, and I'm not sure which one, but probably a man named O'Toole, decided that they had to kill everyone or they'd be fingered."

"That's what the woman said?"

"Those are almost exactly her words. When that statement was made, the bank manager, Mr. Madison, realized that he had no choice but to pull his derringer and then try to reach a rifle in his office. After that, Miss Peterson doesn't remember much of anything other than all the noise and terror.

"Her exact words were 'When those young and brave deputies realized that something terrible was going to happen, they had no choice but to draw their guns and open fire at close quarters.'"

Mayor Plummer swallowed hard and stood up. "Excuse me for a moment," he said, reaching for his handkerchief and stepping just out of the office to blow his nose and wipe tears from his eyes.

Longarm whispered to his boss. "Did the mayor have any more news on his son's condition?"

"Yes. Henry was going to make it, but he'll be in the hospital for weeks and he may never make a full recovery."

"Damn," Longarm said. "I'm sorry to hear that. I was hoping he'd make a full and complete recovery."

Mayor Flannery stepped back into the office. "I'm going to have one of my assistants meet and talk with Miss Agnes Peterson. If her story is exactly as you've told me, I'll need a short time in order to decide just how responsible you two are for that bank slaughter."

When Billy just nodded, Longarm could not hold his tongue any longer. "Mayor, I like your son; he's everything any man could want in a son. Having said that, however, I wasn't comfortable with him becoming a lawman, but that was what he wanted and he promised to follow my orders to the letter and vowed that he would not lose his nerve in a fight."

Longarm paused, trying to read the mayor's reaction. When he failed to do that, he added, "Henry was true to his word in that bank, and I am convinced that he and Deputy Flannery did everything humanly possible to save as many innocent lives as possible."

The mayor stuffed his handkerchief into his pocket. "Marshal, I understand what you are trying to tell me. But the fact of the matter is that a United States deputy marshal died yesterday, as well as a bank manager and several other innocent people. That is absolutely *not* acceptable!"

"Perhaps not," Longarm replied, his voice hardening. "But this isn't a perfect world, and nothing works exactly as it is supposed to all the time."

"Too many lives were lost or possibly ruined."

"And saved," Longarm snapped. "Mayor, do you know the *real* reason that your son wanted to be a lawman?"

The mayor was momentarily caught off guard by the question and blurted, "Of course! When my son was just a lad in Baltimore, he witnessed the horror of watching his mother and a policeman being shot to death in the street. It took Henry years before he could even speak of that terrible and murderous act. And so I believe my son has always felt a strong . . . even overpowering . . . commitment to get criminals off the street and to see that justice and the law of our land are upheld."

"That's right," Longarm said. "Henry did take on the oath of office and assumed the responsibilities of being a lawman to uphold the law. But he had another reason, and that was that he had learned that the men who murdered his mother had come to Denver."

"I know that! I hired a first-rate detective to try and track them down, and after a year he tendered his report saying that the murderers were brothers named Dirk and Harold Raney and that they had either changed their names or left Denver, most likely the latter. My detective followed every lead and finally told me that their trail had vanished and that there was no way to ever bring them to justice."

Longarm glanced at Billy, then made his decision. "Mayor, I understand how you feel about what happened yesterday, and your anger is completely justified. But if you take no retaliatory action against my boss or myself, who were only trying to bring a vicious gang to justice, then I will make you one solemn promise."

The mayor could not hide his surprise. "What kind of promise?"

"I'll find and bring the two men who murdered your wife and the mother of your son to justice."

"How can you *possibly* make such a promise?"

Longarm reached into his vest pocket, removed his

badge, and placed it into the palm of the mayor's hand. "If I don't arrest and return those killers here for trial with their full confession, then you can toss my badge in the garbage. But if I do bring them back, dead or alive, you will not only give me back my badge, but you will take no action against the best man that I have ever had the privilege of working for, Marshal Billy Vail."

Billy's hands shot up in protest. "Custis, I won't allow you to—"

"It's done," Longarm said, eyes never leaving those of the mayor. "I can't restore Henry Plummer to full health, but I can make restitution for what happened so long ago on the streets of Baltimore."

The mayor took a deep breath and rubbed his jaw thoughtfully. "I won't condone you executing two men under any circumstances."

"I won't execute them," Longarm promised. "But I'll track them down, and then they can either surrender or fight. If they choose to fight rather than come back here for a trial, then they risk dying . . . same as I will." Longarm pushed back his coat to reveal the butt of his big Colt. "I can't make it any cleaner or clearer to you than that, Mayor Plummer."

"No," the mayor said quietly, "you've made it pretty clear."

Longarm extended his hand. "Then do we have a deal?"

The mayor shook hands. "I'll keep this badge of yours, and if you don't do as you promised . . . then I'll expect you to resign, just as I'll expect a resignation from Marshal Vail."

Longarm nodded, and when he looked at his boss, he wasn't sure what the man was thinking.

"If you'll excuse me," Longarm said to them both, "I'm not going to waste any more time. Mayor, tell your son that I am extremely proud of him. Tell Henry that he acted every bit as bravely as any United States federal marshal could ever be expected to act."

"I'll tell him that," the mayor promised. "Good luck, *Citizen* Long."

"Billy," Longarm said, turning to his friend and boss, "I won't be back until this is finished."

"I understand. But if you need any help, any help at all, just come back here and I'll do what I can."

"Thanks," Longarm said on his way out the door.

What had he done? He was no longer a federal officer. He was a lone wolf on a lone hunt that was going to end in somewhere he could not yet even imagine, and it was going to end with blood being shed. And he was going to be hunting that ending up a very, very cold trail.

Chapter 13

Longarm waited a few moments, until Denver's Sheriff Clyde Lanier was finished with some business, and then was motioned into the man's office. "Sheriff, I could sure use your help."

Lanier was a big, congenial man in his forties with a walrus mustache and three chins under his prominent jaw. Grossly overweight but with a keen intelligence, he was respected by his peers and well liked by all but Denver's criminal element. "Yeah, after yesterday and that bank holdup fiasco, I'm sure that you can. You should have brought me and my people in on it, Custis. We're not too damn happy with you feds right now."

"I apologize, but it is a *federally chartered bank*, and I know how stretched you are with all the cases and trouble you're buried under."

"Don't try to soft-pedal this," Lanier warned. "I don't like to find out that a local bank turned into a battleground and then have reporters hounding me for answers."

"I'm sure that Marshal Vail would be happy to set up a meeting and—"

"It's not your boss that concerns me," Lanier interrupted. "It's the mayor! I didn't even know his kid had pinned on one of your badges, much less that you'd be sending him into an ambush."

"It wasn't an 'ambush.'" Longarm took a couple of minutes to patiently explain what had happened and how it had all gone wrong in the bank. He finished by saying, "And we've met with the mayor, and he now understands that his son and Deputy Flannery were suddenly caught in a terrible situation and had no choice but to go for their guns."

When Longarm finished his explanation, Lanier laced his thick fingers behind his head and smiled rather sadly. "I'm sure glad that I'm not working for Billy Vail right now. This whole town is outraged by the slaughter that took place in that bank."

"I understand."

"So what kind of a favor do you need? A job here? If that's it, Custis, you're hired."

For the first time since entering the man's office, Longarm managed to smile. "I thank you for that, Sheriff, but I'm after something very different."

"Let's hear it then." The sheriff glanced at a clock. "I've got a meeting in about ten minutes."

"This won't take that much time," Longarm assured the man. "Are you aware that Mayor Flannery's wife was murdered on the streets of Baltimore sixteen or so years ago?"

"Yes. That's a commonly known fact."

"Well," Longarm said, "the murderers were never found."

"I know that, too," Lanier said. "The mayor hired detectives, and they hounded me for information about a pair of brothers named . . . I forget, but that were supposed to be working in Denver. We did what we could to be of assistance, not for the private detectives but for the mayor, who is a personal friend."

"I see," Longarm mused. "Well, then I'm probably wasting our time, both of us, because I was hoping you might have someplace for me to start on that case."

The sheriff scowled. "Why on earth are you, a *federal officer*, messing around with an old local Baltimore murder case?"

"Long story made short; I promised the mayor that if he would take the heat off my boss and myself, I'd repay him by tracking down the killers of his wife and a Baltimore policeman who was also gunned down in the street when Henry Plummer was just a boy."

Lanier leaned forward and laid his meaty forearms on his desk. "You *promised* the mayor you'd do that?"

"It was the only thing that I could think of to do in repayment for the way our office messed up."

"And he agreed?"

"When Mayor Plummer learned that our deputies had no choice but to go for their guns or watch people start being executed inside the bank, he began to understand that what had happened was inevitable. But I still felt responsible, and so what I did was to offer him some restitution in exchange."

"Restitution or revenge?"

"Call it what you want, the result will probably be the same if I find them—and I *will* find them."

The sheriff rolled his eyes to the ceiling, leaned far back in his chair, and thought about what he'd just heard, before turning back to Longarm. "Do you know how much money Mayor Plummer paid detectives to find those murderers?"

"No, and I really don't care."

"He paid them a small *fortune*. They were the best of the best, and not one of them came up with so much as a lead on where those brothers that murdered Mrs. Plummer long ago had gone to ground. The mayor hired former Pinkerton agents . . . real professionals."

"Did they leave any files?"

"No. Nothing."

"Did they . . . Did they tell you anything about what they had found?"

"Only that the brothers were skilled reinsmen. They were mule skinners first and foremost but also teamsters. They were supposed to be very good, but when jobs were short they were quite competent as horseshoers. And when even that kind of employment was unavailable, they would work as stablemen. Naturally, every stable, freighting company, and stagecoach company was contacted, but nothing came of that."

"Were the brothers rounders or troublemakers?"

"Not that I know of. We never arrested a pair of brothers like that."

"Did the detectives hear that they were married or had lasting relationships with women?"

The sheriff shrugged. "They were whoremongers. They drank and spent their money on wild women."

"Were they gamblers?"

"Not that I heard."

"What did they look like?"

Sheriff Lanier shrugged. "The only descriptions that were ever given were from Henry, and those was from a young boy who was probably scared witless. He remembered that the brothers were of average height. Black hair and full beards, and that they were ugly and dirty. I'm afraid that Henry is the only one that ever actually saw the Raney brothers."

"I wonder if that is even their name."

"Probably not." Lanier came to his feet. "I'm sorry that I can't help you more than that."

Longarm shook the man's hand and had started to leave, when Lanier said, "Oh, one thing you may or may not know."

"Yeah?"

"After the former Pinkerton men left Denver with nothing, I fired a young hotheaded deputy named Horatio Manatee, and he went straight to the mayor and offered his services in helping find the brothers so that they could be brought to a long overdue justice."

"And?"

"Mayor Plummer explained to Horatio Manatee that he'd hired the best detectives but that if Horatio wanted to try and find the brothers and bring them to a long overdue justice, he would pay five thousand dollars for them dead . . . or alive."

"And what did Horatio Manatee do?"

"About a month after he started looking for the brothers, he wound up being murdered in the rough railroad town of Rawlins, Wyoming. I only learned of it because one of the papers found on Manatee's body had my forged name on it saying he was an authorized Denver deputy. And that angered more than saddened me."

"What happened after that?"

"I have no idea. Manatee had a young woman he wanted to marry. She was a beauty and I forget her name, but I passed the information of Manatee's death on to her and she seemed to take it pretty hard."

"Any chance you could help me find her?"

The sheriff nodded. "You know, I think I have her name in a file out in the front office. Have one of my men look it up under 'Manatee.' I kept some papers, and I believe that the address of Horatio's intended wife can be found in that file."

"Thanks, Sheriff."

"You owe me one," the man said. "And you can repay me by doing what no one else could do . . . find those bastard brothers if they are still alive and put them six feet underground, or leave them hanging from a tall tree."

"That I will damn sure try to do."

"See that you do and all will be forgiven not only by me, but by my friend Mayor Plummer."

"Understood," Longarm said with his mind already on that Horatio Manatee file that rested in a cabinet almost within his reach.

Chapter 14

Longarm stood in the front office while a clerk slowly thumbed through the file cabinets looking for the one marked "Manatee." Suddenly, there was a commotion at the front door and a deputy was trying to drag a very intoxicated man into the office to be booked and sent to a cell.

"Excuse me," the clerk said. "Deputy Morrison looks like he could use my help."

"I'll just go ahead and finish looking through this file cabinet," Longarm offered.

Distracted and harried, the clerk nodded and went to help the officer, who was by now barely holding his own in a full-blown fistfight. Seeing this as a great opportunity, Longarm quickly started going through the file cabinet and soon found what he was looking for. He opened the Manatee file and there was a letter addressed to a Miss Milly Ott. The letter had her address neatly printed on the front, and because it had not been postmarked, Longarm knew that it had never been sent or even opened. No doubt someone had intended it to be delivered to Milly Ott but had forgotten and so the letter had remained in the file.

I wonder if there is something inside that might give me valuable information, Longarm thought.

He frowned as he picked up and studied the letter. It was against his principles to open what was probably a love letter between two people who were strangers to him. On the other hand, the return address showed him that the letter had been written from a rooming house in Rawlins, Wyoming, and so he knew that it might contain some really important information.

Longarm slipped Milly Ott's letter into his coat pocket. He glanced through the remainder of the thin file, seeing nothing of interest, and returned it to the filing cabinet.

The clerk and the deputy had finally subdued the big brawler, and now the clerk came back, out of breath and looking disheveled. "You found the file, huh?"

"Yeah," Longarm said. "Not much in there, I'm afraid."

"We should probably just throw it out. How old is it?"

"I have no idea."

"There is a date on the inside of the cover. If it's over two years, we toss it, but that's one of those little jobs that I never quite get around to doing."

"Sure," Longarm said. "Thanks for your help. That drunk looked like a mean one, and he's quite a handful."

The clerk watched the first officer and another who had just shown up manhandle the big drunk down a hallway toward the back of the building, which was a block of cells. "Ormly gets that way every few weeks and beats the hell out of someone and gets himself arrested. We jail him for about a week and then have no choice but to turn him loose. One of these days Ormly is either going to get himself shot . . . or he'll beat someone to death, and then he'll either hang or go to prison."

"You're right," Longarm agreed as he headed outside.

Once on the street, he removed the letter from his pocket, opened it and read the contents, which were brief.

Dear Milly,

I think I've found them murdering brothers! Not sure but most likely the Raney pair and they don't know who I am. I plan to do a little more digging here and when I've got enough information I'm going to get the drop on them and then it'll be over. I'd rather kill them and take them back to Denver, but either way I'll get the reward and we can get married and have a good life together. Maybe the sheriff will even offer to give me my old job back, but I might not take it. I'll send this letter later today and be in your arms and bed damn soon and we can roll in all that cash that Mayor Plummer will pay me. Sure can't wait to get some of your red-hot lovin'!

Your soon-to-be husband
Horatio

Longarm reread the letter and then noted the address. It was very possible that Milly had moved but certainly worth a chance that he'd find her, and she might have received an earlier letter that would give him some more information about the Raney brothers.

Longarm knew exactly where Milly Ott lived, and he wasted no time in walking over to her neighborhood at the east end of the town. It was an average, working class neighborhood, and for the most part the houses were neat and well tended.

When he stopped in front of Milly's house, he saw that it was one of the nicer ones, with a comfortable front porch. There was a sign on the front fence that advertised sewing, custom dressmaking, and drapery. The walk leading up to the house had been shoveled, and there seemed to be a light on inside, so Longarm went up to the door and knocked.

A moment passed before the door opened a crack and Longarm was face-to-face with a young and attractive woman with red hair and freckles across the bridge of her upturned nose.

"May I help you?" she asked.

"I'm hoping so."

"Do you have a shirt or something that needs mending? I'm kind of backed up today on some drapery for a woman who is in quite a hurry, but . . ."

"I'm not here for your sewing services," he said, reaching into his vest pocket for his badge and only then remembering he'd handed it over to the mayor. "Uh . . . I work for the federal marshal's office, and

I'm here to ask you a few questions about Mr. Horatio Manatee."

Her smile evaporated. "He was murdered in Rawlins, Wyoming, some time ago, so . . ."

"I know that, Miss Ott. I just left the sheriff's office, and he told me about Mr. Manatee and how he was trying to find a vicious pair of murderers for the mayor."

"That's right, but what does this have to do with anything after all this time?"

"I'm also looking for the Raney brothers."

"I see." She studied him closely. "Do you work for Sheriff Lanier?"

"No. I'm a federal marshal."

"May I see your badge or some identification?"

"I, uh, gave the mayor my badge just this morning. But if you want, I can get a letter or something so you know that I'm really a law officer. Or you could come down with me to the Federal Building and . . ."

"I don't have time to do anything of the sort, Mr. . . ."

"Mr. Long. I really need to talk to you, Miss Ott, about what Horatio Manatee found in Rawlins."

"I don't know what he found, other than an untimely death. You see, he wanted to marry me."

"And you *didn't* want to marry him?"

"I was . . . was considering it. Horatio was handsome and charming, intelligent, and he could be very sweet, but . . ."

"But what, Miss Ott?"

"He had a very violent temper. It was quick and

then it was gone. His temper got him into trouble at the sheriff's office, and there were times when I found him to be . . . well, frightening."

"Maybe his temper got him killed in Rawlins."

"I expect that is exactly what happened," Milly Ott said, folding her arms across her bosom. "Anyway, I grieved for Horatio. I had hopes that in time he would learn to control his temper, find a suitable occupation, and become a very good and steady man. Unfortunately, he wasn't given that time."

"I sure do need to talk to you, Miss Ott, and I promise to be brief."

She cocked an eyebrow. "And you *really* are a federal officer of the law?"

"I swear it. I'm just on kind of a temporary absence."

"If that is the case, then why are you here?"

"I want to find and bring the Raney brothers to a way overdue justice. As you know, they murdered the mayor's wife long ago. The mayor's son is now a deputy, and I want to help him find the men who murdered his mother long ago in Baltimore."

"For the five-thousand-dollar reward, I'm sure."

"No," Longarm said. "For reasons more complicated. May I come in for a few minutes? I have something that belongs to you."

"To me?"

"Yes." Longarm took out the letter that he'd taken from the sheriff's office and showed it to the young woman but did not hand it to her.

"Come in," she said. "If I don't take the time with you, I'll be distracted by curiosity all day."

"I'd imagine that would be a problem if you're mending things and making drapes."

"Yes, it would be." Milly Ott opened the door and allowed Longarm entrance. She pointed to a chair and asked, "I have a pot of tea brewing, would you like a cup?"

"I thought you were in a big hurry."

"I am, but I can work while we talk. But first, I want to see that letter. Is it from Horatio?"

"Yes. He wrote it before he died in Rawlins."

"Oh, dear. I'm not sure that I want to read it until I'm alone. I might cry and then we'd both be embarrassed."

"I understand." Longarm gave her the letter. "But I sure need to know if Horatio Manatee sent you any letters after this one that would give me some information."

"The letter has been opened," she said, looking up at him sharply. "Did *you* open and read it?"

"I did."

"You shouldn't have."

"I had to, Miss Ott."

Milly Ott sighed and read the brief letter. Longarm closely watched her expression, and he read the gamut of emotions she was experiencing. When she was through with the letter, she handed it back to Longarm.

"I don't need it," he said. "You can keep it."

In reply, Milly walked over to a little potbellied stove that was burning and tossed the letter inside.

She clasped her hands together and came right up to Longarm. "That might have seemed callous, but the truth is that I believe we should put the past in the past. I have kept the things of my late mother because I loved her very much and miss her. I burned everything of my late father's because he was a beast and an uncouth lout."

Longarm took a seat. "What else besides that letter can you tell me about Horatio Manatee and what he found in Rawlins?"

She sat down across from him on a nice sofa and said, "I'm sure now that I've read that letter that Horatio really did find those brothers. And I'm quite sure that it was they who murdered him when he tried to arrest them."

"Did Horatio say anything else in an earlier letter that would help me find the brothers?"

"As a matter of fact, he did. The very last letter that I received from him before the one you just showed me said that the brothers had told some people that they were leaving Rawlins and heading to Nevada, to work for a big company that was hauling ore out of some mines."

"Do you remember the name of the town in Nevada?"

"It was Gold Hill." She looked at him. "Have you ever heard of such a place?"

"Yes. It's on the Comstock Lode right below Virginia City. Both towns have seen their best days in terms of silver and gold, but I'm sure that there are still a number of mines operating at a profit."

"Well," Milly said with a shrug, "that's what I remember Horatio writing to tell me from Rawlins."

"I don't suppose you kept the . . ."

"No, I burned it, the same way I burned the one you

just gave me." She stood up and put her hands on her hips. "I'm a woman who tries hard to always look forward and never backward. Nothing in the world can be gained by looking to your past with regrets or even pride."

"I'll try to remember that." Longarm picked up his hat and started for the door. "I've taken up enough of your time."

"Are you married, Mr. Long?"

"What?" He wasn't sure he'd heard her correctly.

"I asked if you are married."

"Nope. I've always been a bachelor."

"And as handsome as you are, I'll just bet you've broken your share of hearts."

He blushed. "I never set out to break a heart, but it might have happened a time or two."

"Are you engaged or have a steady girl?"

"Nope."

"Are you leaving for Gold Hill, Nevada?"

Longarm had to grin. "You sure do ask a man a lot of questions."

Milly set down her work and came over to him. "If you are a free and unencumbered man and I am a free and unencumbered woman, perhaps we ought to have a farewell dinner together this evening."

"And why would we do that?"

"Because, given just a little time, a good meal with fine wine, I might even remember something that would be very helpful to you in finding the Raney brothers."

Longarm shook his head and smiled. "You are a very direct and puzzling woman, Milly."

"And you are a very handsome and interesting man. So, are you taking me to dinner . . . or not?"

"I am," he said. "And I'll be by to pick you up about seven."

"Make it a *nice* dinner, Mr. Long. I love shrimp and expensive chilled French white wines."

"I'm a poor, underpaid deputy, not a banker."

"You've got to pay the price to enjoy the ride, Mr. Long."

"Call me Custis," he said. "See you at seven."

"Be prompt."

"I will be."

"Then we will have a very enjoyable evening, I promise you."

Longarm was grinning when he left Milly's house. He marveled at how she had been so cold and suspicious when he'd first knocked on her door and even after he'd gone into her home. But something had changed when she'd read and then burned Horatio Manatee's letter. Longarm had no idea what had changed the woman from cold to hot . . . but that was looking back, and tonight was all about looking forward.

Chapter 15

The Frontier House in downtown Denver specialized in steak and shrimp dinners and was known for its excellent wine cellar. Now, with the remnants of ravaged steak and shrimp on their plates, Longarm killed their second bottle of French Pinot Noir and signaled the waiter for a check. He knew that the price was going to be hefty, but on the other hand he was pretty sure that a night with Milly Ott would be exceptional.

"It was a *lovely* meal," Milly said, her eyes a little glazed and her voice a bit slurred from the wine. "And now I think we should go for a walk and clear our heads."

"As long as our walk ends up in your bed," Longarm said with a lecherous smile. "And remember, it's freezing cold out there and the ice makes walking pretty treacherous."

"Ah, yes," she agreed. "You're right. Will you signal the waiter to call for a horse and carriage?"

Longarm nodded, although he would have preferred saving that extra three dollars. But what the hell, in for a penny . . . in for a pound.

"Waiter!"

When the man appeared, Longarm paid the check and asked for the waiter to step outside and signal a horse carriage and driver.

"Was everything to your satisfaction, Marshal Long?" the man asked with an ingratiating smile.

"It was perfect," Longarm said, "and . . ."

Just then, out of the corner of his eye, he saw Mrs. Delia Flannery enter the restaurant with none other than Mayor Tom Plummer. Longarm clucked his tongue. "My oh my," he said with wonder. "Milly, would you just look at that!"

The mayor must have been a regular at the Frontier House, because as he escorted the young and beautiful widow through the room, he was greeted by everyone and shook hands with most of them.

"That's our *mayor*, isn't it?" Milly asked.

"Sure is."

"Is that his daughter? She's really beautiful."

"She is the wife of our late deputy marshal, Mike Flannery," Longarm told her. "He was killed in that bank holdup along with several others. He was a fine man."

"Well," Milly said, "his young widow sure doesn't look like she's deep into mourning."

Longarm would have had to say that Milly was right. Delia Flannery wasn't dressed in black but instead wore a nice white evening dress with a yellow bow in her pretty hair. She was smiling and looked ravishing as the mayor introduced her to his friends.

Suddenly the mayor spotted Longarm and came directly over to his table. "Well, Custis Long, this is about the last place I thought we'd next meet. And your lovely companion is . . ."

"This is Miss Milly . . ." Longarm blushed with embarrassment. "What is your last name?"

"Ott," Milly said. "I'm Miss Milly Ott."

The mayor bowed slightly. "My pleasure. And Custis, good to see that you're hard at work."

"I'm enjoying myself tonight . . . just as you appear to be, Mayor Plummer."

"Miss Flannery and I have just returned from the hospital, where we were visiting my son."

"And how is Henry?"

"He's making a remarkable recovery but very concerned about his leg," the mayor said. "He wonders if it will force him to retire from his short-lived law enforcement career with your office."

Longarm shrugged and tried to offer some encouragement. "I'm sure that after a few months your son will make the right decision."

"I hope so," the mayor replied. "I have some very nice opportunities that Henry could undertake. Things that would be . . . good for my son's future aspirations in this town."

"As opposed to Henry carrying a badge and getting shot."

"Exactly. And I might as well tell you that I've decided to hire Mrs. Flannery as my special assistant."

Longarm looked at the widow with a slightly upraised eyebrow. "Congratulations."

"Thank you," Delia Flannery said. "It's a little

overwhelming to go back to work and especially for the mayor. But when Henry suggested to his father that I would be a wonderful addition to his father's staff . . ."

"So it was Deputy Plummer's idea," Longarm said. "Well, if he can think that clearly, he must not be in too much pain."

"Henry is very brave . . . just like my late husband. I told him that even though he might limp for the rest of his life, that should prove no handicap to doing whatever he decides to do."

Longarm nodded with understanding. He could see far enough into the future to realize that Henry Plummer would never return to becoming a federal or local law officer. Instead, with the badge of a limp to show the world and voters that he was brave and battle-tested, he would probably have a great advantage among voters. It was intriguing that Henry Plummer had suggested to his father that he hire the beautiful and recently widowed Mrs. Delia Flannery. Having accepted the offer, Delia would now be in close contact with young Henry, and it didn't take a crystal ball to predict that that would lead to romance and possibly even marriage.

"Delia, I'm happy for you," Longarm said, meaning it.

"She'll be a great asset to my office," the mayor predicted. "Now, if you'll excuse us, we will have something to eat. Delia and I have been at the hospital all day with Henry, and we're famished."

"Of course," Longarm said. "Good to see you again so soon, Mayor."

"And may I still expect satisfactory results regarding your promise to find the Raney brothers, who murdered my wife and a policeman in Baltimore?"

"Count on it," Longarm said, holding up his empty bottle of white wine. "And actually, this beautiful lady that is with me tonight just happens to know a thing or two about the Raney brothers."

The mayor spun around and his jaw almost dropped. His eyes darted back and forth between Longarm and Milly, and it was clear that he was dying to know more. "Is that so?"

"Yes. You see, Mayor, this lovely woman with me tonight was betrothed to a former United States deputy marshal named Horatio Manatee. I'm sure that you remember him very well."

The mayor paled slightly. "Yes, Horatio came to me with a proposition. He vowed that he would find and either arrest or kill the Raney brothers in return for a reward of five thousand dollars. Unfortunately, I understand that he was murdered somewhere in Wyoming."

"In Rawlins, to be exact. But not before he wrote Milly a few letters that held very important information."

"Did he actually find the brothers!" The mayor could not contain his excitement, and his voice rose so loudly that other diners turned and stared.

"Yes, and there is little doubt that they murdered him, but not before Horatio Manatee wrote some very interesting letters to Milly."

"Saying where they were going next?" the mayor asked, bending close to Longarm.

"I'm not certain, but I have a good idea," Longarm told the man.

Mayor Plummer straightened, and aware that he was creating a lot of interest from other diners, he cleared his throat, regained his composure, and said, "Despite what was agreed upon earlier between us and your superior at the Federal Building, I'll sweeten the pot and offer you the same deal I offered this lady's late fiancé: Find and either arrest those two murderers and bring them back for a trial with their written confessions . . . or kill them. Either way, you'll earn five thousand dollars."

Longarm felt the wine firing his blood. He liked Mayor Plummer and had great respect for young Henry, but his lawman's code was now being put to the test. "I'm not a judge, jury, and hangman all rolled up into one package, Mayor Plummer. I can't kill those men for money."

"Sure you can."

The mayor laid a hand on Longarm's shoulder and whispered, "*I have your badge.* You're no longer an officer of the law, and you can do what you damn well please when you find those murdering sons of bitches. So bring me back their ears and make yourself more reward money from me than you'd be paid in years of salary risking your life every day as a federal marshal."

Longarm locked eyes with the mayor. "I'll find them and get you some restitution, Mayor. Of that you can be very sure."

"And what about the reward? Will you be too high and mighty to accept that?"

Overhearing them, Milly hiccupped and said, "Mayor Plummer, if Custis won't take it . . . I damn sure will!"

The mayor looked at her for a moment, and then he chuckled. "And that would be just fine with me. Perfectly justifiable since they also murdered your man." He took her arm and led her to a corner of the room where they could talk in private. "Milly, can you keep a secret?"

"Of course."

"I don't ever want to see the men that murdered my lovely wife. So if you were considering going along with Custis Long, I would very much appreciate it if you would make sure that my deep desire to see them dead is . . . well, fulfilled."

Milly stared at him. "You're asking me to make sure they die?"

"If it is within your capability . . . yes."

"And what would my . . . 'capability' we worth to you, Mayor?"

"Another five thousand dollars." He smiled. "But please keep this our little secret. I'm afraid that even though I have Custis's badge, he will try to do what he has sworn to do, and that is to bring them in for a trial. I absolutely don't want that. It would cause me a lot of pain and also be very damaging to my son, who has more than enough sadness and personal challenges to deal with right now."

"I understand."

"I wouldn't even suggest such a thing, but I sense in you someone who would do what is right for me and my son."

"I'll think about it," Milly said. "Very hard."

"Please do," the mayor said as he squeezed her arm and left to rejoin Delia, who was waiting at another table.

"So," Milly said, kissing Longarm's cheek. "Do you need some help in Gold Hill?"

"I almost always work alone."

"And what about the five thousand dollars the mayor will pay in a reward? Did you mean what you said about giving it all to me?"

"I'm a bit tipsy, but that's *not* what I just said."

Milly cocked her head a little to one side and giggled. "Tell you what, handsome, let's get out of here and back to my house and I'll help you refresh your memory."

"I'm not sure that it will work that way."

"I am," she told him, as under the table her hand slipped along his thigh to his crotch. "I'm very sure of it."

An hour later, Longarm was ready to agree to almost anything as Milly bounced up and down on his rod, a bottle of brandy in one hand and one of her big breasts cupped in the other.

Longarm looked up at the beautiful woman and laced his hands around the small of her back. "Come down here and roll over, Milly. It's my turn to be on top for a while."

Milly hooted and did as he asked, while taking a big swig of brandy. She was laughing and having a wonderful time, and so was he.

Longarm entered her to the hilt and whispered, "Think you can do it tomorrow?"

"Do this?"

"No, sew a straight seam on a dress or a drapery."

For some reason, Milly thought that was about the

funniest question she'd ever heard in her life, and she began to laugh hysterically. Longarm thought it was funny as well, but he would have bet most anything that Milly wouldn't be steady enough in the morning to even thread a cup handle, much less the eye of a needle.

Chapter 16

Longarm awoke the next morning to find Milly Ott cooking a good breakfast of pancakes, eggs, and bacon. She was dressed, her hair was combed, and she looked surprisingly chipper considering the long night of lovemaking they'd enjoyed.

"Well," Milly said with a smile, "I was wondering when you were going to wake up and have some breakfast."

"Any coffee made?"

"Sure," Milly said. "But you're going to have to get out of bed to enjoy it."

Longarm ran his fingers through his hair and yawned.

"Got to keep up your strength, Big Boy."

Longarm grinned and found his pants. "How come you seem to be in such good spirits after so little sleep last night?"

"Because I had me some good lovin' and because I've come to a very important decision early this morning."

"One I need to know about?"

"I think so," she said. "But it's not one that I'm sure you want to hear."

Longarm took an offered cup of coffee and moved over to Milly's small kitchen table. "I don't like surprises."

"Well, I'm sorry about that," she said, handing him a full breakfast plate. "But maybe you won't mind this surprise too much. What I've decided to do is to join you when you go to Gold Hill, Nevada."

"What!" He had been about to sip coffee, but now Longarm lowered the cup to the table. "Did I hear you right?"

"You sure did. I'm going with you."

Longarm shook his head. "That isn't going to work out for us, Milly. I told you before that I work and travel alone. And besides, you've got a thriving business here in your house."

"I barely get by on what I make sewing and mending. I'm going to tell all my customers this morning that I'm taking a break and that they'll have to take their mending needs elsewhere."

"Milly, I . . ."

"I'm going to Gold Hill, Custis, and before this is all said and done, you'll be damn glad that I came along with you."

"I can't imagine that."

Milly came over and kissed his cheek. "And there's one more thing."

"I'm not sure that I can stand any more of your surprises."

"You might like this one."

"Shoot."

Milly grinned. "I'm almost certain that I've seen the Raney brothers, and won't that be a one helluva big help when we get to the Comstock Lode?"

Longarm stopped chewing. "Yeah, it would mean a lot, but how could that be?"

"Horatio pointed them out to me one afternoon when we were downtown shopping for something. I remember him saying that he'd been doing a lot of hunting and he'd narrowed things down to where he was sure that he was looking at the Raney brothers. He was shaking with excitement and already talking about how to take them or kill them and then go collect his reward from our mayor."

"But the brothers lit out for Rawlins."

"Sure they did . . . they left the day after we saw them parading around with a couple of whores on First Street. They are big men, Custis. Not as big as yourself, but big and ugly. Black beards, closely spaced black eyes. When they saw Horatio looking at them, they stared right back and I felt a chill go up and down my spine. I kind of think they knew that he had recognized them and that's why they left town so suddenly."

Longarm finally drank some coffee. "Would you remember them if you saw them today?"

"Of course." Milly took a chair across from him. "They had the look of Satan on them. I would pick them out in a crowd without hesitation."

"Why don't you tell me exactly what they look like and let that help me when I go to Nevada."

"Nope. I'm going, too."

Longarm pushed a forkful of pancake into his mouth and chewed thoughtfully. "Milly, I'm beginning to believe that this has *everything* to do with what the mayor said privately to you last night in the Frontier Hotel's dining room."

"It might."

"How much money did he offer you?"

"The same amount as he offered you, Custis."

"Another five thousand dollars?"

"That's right." Milly got up and folded her arms across her chest. "And if I help you kill them, I'll earn every penny."

Longarm sighed. "Tell you what. If I kill them or bring them back for trial, I'll only keep my expenses and you can have the rest of the mayor's reward."

"Nope. The mayor will pay us *both* five thousand dollars. Custis, do you know what we could do for ourselves with *ten thousand dollars*?"

"A lot, I suppose. But I'm pretty satisfied doing what I'm doing right now."

"Have you thought about how you run a big risk every time you go after someone? And how as you get older, you won't be as quick or strong? Do you want to end up behind a desk like the man you work for?"

"I have to admit that I'd hate being a paper pusher."

"Then you really need to consider us having a partnership and the opportunities we could have with a ten-thousand-dollar stake."

Longarm needed some time to consider everything

that this woman had laid upon him in a big heap, and so he focused on his breakfast and discovered he was famished.

"Well," Milly said, "are we working together . . . or will we travel separately to Nevada and do what the mayor wants done? *Deserves* to have done?"

"You aren't going to let go of this, are you?"

"No. I've worked hard all my life. Supported some rotten and worthless men. After staring at a needle and thread all day for years, my eyes are starting to weaken and I'm getting older."

"Not that I could tell last night in your bed."

"Don't try and flatter me out of what I've decided, Custis. I'm going, and I promise you that I'll prove to be worth my salt."

He studied her face and judged that she was about as determined as anyone he'd come across in many a day. "All right, Milly. But we need to leave on the train tomorrow morning."

She beamed. "I'll wrap up things with all my customers. I've a friend who is trying to get her mending business off the ground and really needs the money. She'll be very grateful to take all the mending work that I pass over to her."

"Well, good for your friend."

"Don't be upset with me, Custis. I'm a good person and this is my chance. It's *our* chance if you want it to be. With ten thousand dollars and what this house would bring me and what we have saved . . ."

"Whoa up there! The sad truth of the matter is that I don't have much in the way of savings."

"Well, I don't either. I have eight hundred and ten

dollars, last time I checked at the bank. What about you?"

"A little more," he admitted.

"This house is worth almost a thousand. So all together we'd have close to thirteen thousand!"

"Thirteen is an unlucky number," he said around a mouthful. "And we hardly know each other."

"I'd say that after last night we know each other very well. And you *really* like me, don't you?"

He saw the hope in her eyes, and it was easy to tell her the truth. "Yeah, Milly, I like you *a lot*."

"And I like you a lot, too!"

"Well hellfire, then I guess we're going to go to Nevada together and try to find those Raney brothers."

"We'll find them. We just have to find them!"

"They might have kept moving. Men like that get in trouble and wear out their welcome real fast no matter where they go or what they do."

Milly's excitement died. "If they've moved on from Gold Hill, what do we do then?"

"We find out where they lived in Gold Hill and who they worked for and drank with. We talk to the whores they favored, and we gather as much information about them as we possibly can. If it's enough . . . we'll pick up their trail, and it'll be a whole lot fresher than it is right now."

"Good!" Milly pulled on a heavy coat and mittens. "I'm going to go see my friend and tell her she's going to get more additional business than she probably wants or even can handle all at once. Then I'll bring her back, and we'll load up the mending and take it to her house and contact the customers. I'll be all finished with my business today, and we can leave tomorrow."

"Train pulls out at nine-forty-five in the morning," Longarm told her. "Do you have the money for a ticket?"

Milly smiled. "I was kind of hoping that you . . ."

"All right, I'll buy us both tickets, but you'll have to work off that cost on the way out to Reno."

"On my *back* you mean?"

"Or any other way we want it."

She laughed and spun around like a ballerina. "I've never done it on a train."

"It's different with the rocking and bumping across the tracks."

"Is it . . . better?"

It was Longarm's turn to chuckle. "I can't see how it could be better than it was for us last night, but I'll let you be the judge."

Milly came over and hugged his head and then raced for the door. "Dinner tonight at the Frontier Hotel again?"

"Hell yes, let's do a full repeat!"

Longarm was grinning to himself as Milly slammed the door and hurried off to do her business. He just hoped she didn't go too fast down the sidewalk, slip on some ice, and bust her pretty little butt.

Chapter 17

Longarm and Milly had boarded the Denver and Pacific Railroad for Cheyenne the very next day and, when they arrived, taken a room at the Butler House. The next morning, after a nice breakfast and with several hours to wait before they boarded the Union Pacific for Reno, Longarm decided that he should check with the local authorities.

So he left Milly at the hotel and went over to see Marshal Otis Appleton, Cheyenne's current marshal and an old and trusted friend.

"Well, well, if it isn't Custis Long come to pay me a visit," Appleton said with a grin and an outstretched hand. "Good to see you."

"You too," Longarm replied, reaching into his coat pocket. "Cigar?"

"Depends on what you're smoking on this trip. Sometimes you've got Cubans that I'd kill for . . . other times you're smoking stinky cheroots that would gag a maggot. So which is it today?"

"I've got some good cigars from Kentucky. Not the quality of the Cubans, but they're far less expensive and I like them fine."

"Then I'll have one. Sit down, Custis. I've got some hot coffee left over from yesterday. Want a cup?"

"No, thanks. We just had a good breakfast and I've already drank more coffee than usual."

"What's the 'we' you're referring to?"

"Oh," Longarm said, instantly regretting the slip of his tongue. "I'm traveling to Reno with a friend."

"Man or woman?" the marshal asked, a smile of amusement on his craggy face as he lit his cigar.

"Woman."

"Serious about her?"

Longarm lit his own cigar and had to smile. "Jeez, Otis. What are you, a romantic or something?"

"Well, I'm a happily married man, and I just naturally think that my friends ought to have the same happiness and benefits that I enjoy every single day."

"Those benefits being?"

Now it was Otis who smiled and blushed. "Never you mind, Custis. What brings you here and why are you taking a woman all the way to Reno?"

"It's a long story," Longarm answered, "but I'll give you the short version."

In a few minutes Longarm had explained about the Raney brothers and the mayor of Denver's driving desire to have them brought to justice for murdering his wife and a Baltimore policeman many years ago. When he finished, he said, "The woman I'm with can identify the Raney brothers . . . or at least that's what she says."

"I've certainly heard of Mayor Tom Plummer. Never heard anything bad about the man."

"He's a good man, all right. We hired his son to be a federal marshal, and he wasn't on the job but a short time before he was involved in a bank holdup that nearly got him killed. Anyway, I feel kind of responsible for things, and that's why I'm going to hunt down the Raney brothers and either kill them or bring them to justice."

"I see."

"There's one other thing I should tell you," Longarm said, puffing on his cigar. "I voluntarily gave up my badge to do this job."

"But why!"

Longarm studied the ash at the tip of his cigar. "I just felt that it was something I needed to do, so that I could take whatever measures were necessary to bring those brothers to justice."

Marshal Appleton frowned. "I hope you're not planning to just kill those brothers rather than arrest them and see that they get a fair trial."

"I'll do whatever I need to do," Longarm said. "The truth is that it would be almost impossible to get justice for the mayor's murdered wife or that Baltimore policeman after all these years. The only living witness is the mayor's son, and a lot of juries might take into account that he was a very young boy when his mother died and that he could be mistaken."

"I see."

"What I came by here for, in addition to making

sure that you're keeping out of mischief, is to ask if you have ever heard of the Raney brothers. Or arrested them."

"I never arrested anyone by the name of Raney . . . but they might have changed their names."

"They most likely did," Longarm agreed. "And I knew your having arrested them was a long shot, but I felt I needed to ask."

"I did arrest a pair that looked like brothers," the marshal said after a moment. "They had robbed a couple of drunks and beat them up so badly that they almost died. I'd never have caught the pair except that there were a few witnesses who were so shocked at the savagery of the attack that they decided they had to come and report it to me. I took a pair of deputies with me, and we found the pair in a whorehouse across the tracks. They were dead drunk and raising hell, and I had to whip one with my pistol because he was such a brute."

Longarm was suddenly very interested. "Describe them for me, Otis."

"Well, let's see. They were big bastards. Probably each weighed about two-fifty naked. And they were naked when we got the drop on them."

"Clean-shaven or bearded?"

"Bearded. Black beards with some silver in 'em."

"Anything else you remember?"

"No. We handcuffed the pair and let them dress before we brought them over to our cell. They stayed about two days and were bailed out by Jim Stanton, who owns a freighting business down—"

"They're the ones," Longarm interrupted. "The Raney brothers."

"Well," Appleton said, "they didn't tell me anything about being brothers, but they sure looked a lot alike."

"How long ago were they here?"

"Let's see. Maybe a few months ago."

"What name did they give you?"

"I forget. Sorry." Appleton stood up. "But the judge keeps a record of everyone that comes before him. He would have their names written down and filed."

"That would be Judge Quinn?"

"Yep. He's still on the bench and just as crusty as always."

"Can I find him at the courthouse?"

"Sure can."

Longarm came to his feet. "We're catching the westbound, and I believe it pulls out of your town around noon."

"That's right. It's usually right on time, so don't be late and miss traveling with that woman. Is she single and pretty?"

"Yeah, she is."

The marshal of Cheyenne chuckled. "Might be I'll wander down to the train depot just to get a look at her and decide if you're worthy of her, Custis."

"Do that," Longarm said, knowing he was being ribbed and not taking the bait.

"She a *respectable* woman?"

"As respectable as I'd care to travel with," Longarm said, heading out the door.

The courthouse was close by, and Longarm went there directly. After he entered the building, he was taken to see the judge, who greeted him warmly. "How are things down Denver way?" the judge asked.

"They're fine."

"I heard that you people had one hell of a botched up bank robbery."

"Yeah, it was a bad one," Longarm said.

"Heard that the mayor's son was involved."

"You don't miss much, do you, Judge?"

"No, I have a lot of friends in Denver, and you know that I visit my sister there every month or two. I like Denver, but I like Cheyenne better . . . or at least I would if the damned wind wasn't always blowing about fifty miles an hour."

It was a joke, and Longarm laughed. "Judge, I'm here unofficially, and I'm tracking a pair of brothers that Marshal Appleton said he brought before you on charges of drunkenness and serious assault."

"That happens almost every Saturday night in Cheyenne. Can you be more specific?"

Marshal Appleton says that they were brought before your bench a couple of months ago. They were brothers . . . big men with black beards probably in their forties. I have also been told they have a meanness that is hard to miss."

"Oh yes, I remember them now."

"It would help me if you have the names they were using."

"I can provide that from my files."

"I'm leaving for Reno at noon. This pair might be in Rawlins or they might be in Gold Hill on the Comstock Lode."

"Well," the judge said, "they're not here and good

riddance to them. The two men that they beat and robbed were in bad shape for weeks after the attacks. I would have thrown the book at them except they were bailed out and they promised to leave town on the first train."

"I see."

"Let's go into my office and I'll look up the names they used," Judge Quinn said, climbing out of his chair and heading for the office.

Ten minutes later, Longarm had the names that the brothers had used. "Dirk Pierce and Harold York," he said. "Not too creative."

"What were their real names?" the judge asked.

"Dirk and Harold Raney."

"You're right. Not very imaginative." The judge studied his slim file. "Not anything here that I can tell you in addition to the names and their crimes. They listed their occupation as mule skinners, and since they were bailed out by a local freight company, that is probably true."

"It is," Longarm said. "Thanks for your help, Judge."

"I don't know if I was any help at all."

"There is always the chance that they kept those last names when they left town."

Longarm hurried back to the hotel, where Milly was already packed and waiting in the lobby. She looked nervous. "My gosh, Custis, the train is leaving in fifteen minutes!"

"Plenty of time for us to catch it."

"You don't leave much margin for error, do you?"

"Never have," he said, grabbing up their bags and then paying his bill at the hotel counter. By the time that was finished, he glanced at a big old wall clock and saw that the Union Pacific was pulling out in about seven minutes.

They heard the train's whistle for the last call, and then they were racing down the street toward the depot.

"Damn you, Custis, I don't like this!"

"Sorry!"

The train was just starting to move when they hopped on board, gasping for breath.

"I'm not very happy with you," Milly grumped.

"Let's go to our sleeping compartment, where I'll really make you run out of breath," Longarm told her with an impish smile.

Milly blushed and jammed an elbow into his ribs as they moved down the aisle and the train began to pick up speed.

Chapter 18

"I never saw such ugly country in all of my life," Milly declared one morning as their train pulled out of Winnemucca, Nevada, still chugging westward toward Reno, yet 165 miles away. "Can *anything* live out in this high desert?"

"Sure," Longarm said. "Wild mustangs do well out here and so do the Paiute Indians. You'll see jackrabbits. Once in a while a coyote or deer."

"Well, if you say so," Milly replied, "but this is *ugly* country."

"Beauty is in the eye of the beholder," Longarm said. "We're used to the high Rocky Mountains, and there isn't much to compare to them or to the Laramie Mountains. But when we get to Reno, you'll see the Sierra Nevada Mountains, and they're handsome and thick with pine. This time of year there will be a lot of snow up on the peaks and there even may be a good deal in Reno."

"What about on the Comstock Lode?" she asked. "Is it high and green and likely to be covered with snow?"

"No," Longarm told her. "It can snow up on the Comstock, but not too much. It is dotted here and there with a few piñon and juniper pines that survived the miners that came in and basically lumbered off all the timber for their square-set mining and for cabins and campfires. The Comstock Lode sets on Sun Mountain, and you'll rarely see a bleaker or more barren mountain and surrounding country."

"People always go where the gold and silver is to be found, I guess."

"That's right. The Comstock Mines produced one of the greatest bonanzas ever found in America. In fact, I'm sure you've heard of Dan DeQuille and Mark Twain. They were reporters on the Comstock Lode, working for the famous *Territorial Enterprise*, and later DeQuille wrote a huge and popular book called *The Big Bonanza*. It was a fine read, and of course we all know about Mark Twain's great success."

"Yes, but I've never read his work."

"You should someday," Longarm said. "Twain has a wonderful sense of humor and way of describing things; once you get started on his books, they are about impossible to put down."

"Well," Milly said, "mostly I'm just sick of riding this train across a landscape that looks like it stretches all the way out to hell and back."

"We'll be pulling into Reno this evening," he said. "Tomorrow, we'll take a stagecoach up to Virginia City. Gold Hill is just down the other side of the mountain a short distance."

"But you say that the Comstock Lode is on the decline?"

"That's right. The forty-niners swarmed to the gold streams along the western slope of the Sierra Nevada Mountains in the late forties and fifties, and when the California gold camps finally went bust they made this amazing discovery of silver and gold on the Comstock Lode. But while the forty-niners worked rivers and streams with their gold pans, long toms, and sluices, when they came to Nevada to work the Comstock, many were shocked to find that it was all about deep and hard rock mining."

"So how did they get to the ore if it was deep underground?"

"Some dug holes and others hacked out tunnels into the mountains and found some gold and silver. All over the hillsides, you can see little mounds of mine tailings that look like giant gopher piles, but most of the Comstock's wealth was brought up from great depths by steam engines that lowered men and supplies into deep holes in the ground. Some of the biggest mines went down hundreds and hundreds of feet."

"Sounds like it was a terrible life for the miners."

"It was," Longarm agreed. "A lot of miners died on the Comstock, in mine cave-ins, and some hit pockets of boiling water down below and were scalded to death. But most died of pneumonia because they'd come up from the steamy depths hot and sweating and then in winter be hit by the cold, frigid air. That sudden temperature change killed them off like flies."

Longarm remembered all the cemeteries around Virginia City. "You see, the deeper a mine went the hotter it became," he explained. "I was down in one of the mines, and at five hundred feet the temperature was well over a hundred degrees. It was about as tough a place to work as I've ever seen."

"What about Gold Hill?"

"It always competed with Virginia City, and there were some rich mines down in Gold Canyon, but it never became a very large city. Still, I'm sure that there are still mines all over the Comstock Lode that are being worked profitably. It's just that they're not producing nearly what they did in the sixties and even the seventies."

"I sure hope that the Raney brothers are still there."

"Me too," Longarm said. "Or at least that if they aren't there, we can find out where they went next."

"We really need that ten thousand dollars the mayor will pay us."

"I suppose," Longarm said, gazing out the window.

"You don't seem very sure of it."

Longarm shrugged. "I don't know, Milly. I've never had a lot of money or even much of a wish to be wealthy. I live a simple life and make enough as a federal marshal to buy most of what I want or need."

"But wouldn't you like to have a lot of money? Enough money to buy a business or to maybe travel to Europe?"

"Not really."

"Well how about we go to New York City or to New Orleans by floating down the Mississippi River on a paddle-wheel steamer? Doesn't that sound wonderful?"

"Actually, that sounds a lot more fun to me than

traveling to Europe. I'd soon get bored sitting around on an ocean steamship for weeks."

"We have plenty of time to sort it all out," Milly said, slipping her arm through his own. "And I was thinking that we ought to go back to our compartment and enjoy the motion a few more times."

"Ha! You're insatiable."

"Yeah, but don't you love it?"

In reply, Longarm took her hand and led her out of the dining room and down to their small, private, and rocking bed.

"Reno! Next stop is Reno, Nevada!"

Longarm and Milly finished their last bout of energetic lovemaking just as the train pulled into the station. A feeble winter sun was just sinking into the Sierras, and when they grabbed their bags and stepped outside, the temperature was already near freezing.

"It's cold here!" Milly complained, looking around at the snow and ice. "You didn't tell me it would be worse than Denver."

"I don't know if it's worse or not," Longarm said, taking her arm. "Let's go find a hotel room on Virginia Street near the Truckee River."

"As long as it's not too far to walk in this cutting wind and the rooms are heated."

"We'll have a nice dinner at the Domino Hotel, and a few glasses of whiskey and wine will set us up and get the blood warmed in a hurry."

"Lead the way!"

They tromped through the snow and slush with their heads lowered to the icy wind. When they got to the

Domino Hotel, where Longarm had stayed several times in the past, they hurried inside to where a huge stone fireplace was roaring in the lobby and people were seated on fine leather couches and sofa chairs.

"This is really nice," Milly said, admiring the marble floors and high-beamed ceilings. "But isn't it kind of expensive?"

"It is beyond what I normally am willing to pay for," Longarm confessed. "But we've been on a train for three days and nights and I just felt that we needed a little luxury. Besides, the steaks and ribs here are the finest around."

"Any seafood?"

"I'm sure that it's on their menu," Longarm said, leading Milly over to the registration desk, where a slim man waited, with round eyeglasses and slick hair parted right down the middle.

"Good evening!"

"Good evening," Longarm said. "We need a room."

"Of course. We have a few still available. If you'd sign the register, we'll get you taken care of at once."

Longarm signed them in as Mr. and Mrs. Long. Milly noticed and nudged him, whispering, "Now, doesn't that look nice in print?"

"Don't get your hopes up."

Milly laughed. Longarm knew that she wasn't any more interested in getting married right away than he was. They had come all the way to Nevada to carry out what very well might become a deadly showdown. There was just too much yet to be decided to even think about things of permanence.

"The bellboy will escort you up to your room,

which is number two-ten. Will you be eating in our restaurant tonight?"

"We will."

"Shall I make you a reservation right now?"

"Sure," Longarm said, pulling out his railroad watch. "Make it for eight. That will give us time to freshen up."

"Very good, sir."

Longarm and Milly went up to their room, which overlooked the Truckee River. And even though it had gotten dark, there were still enough streetlights to see the river and the bridge that crossed it.

"There is a beautiful walk along the river toward the west. Very popular but not in this kind of weather."

"Maybe another time," she said, slipping into his arms and sliding her hand down into his pants. "Milly, we just did that on the train not more than an hour ago."

"Too weak for a quick repeat?"

Longarm shook his head. "Insatiable," he said, before he kissed her mouth and led her over to their big, wonderful, and bouncy hotel bed.

Chapter 19

"First time going to visit Virginia City?" their handsome and well-dressed fellow passenger asked Longarm and Milly as they settled into the stagecoach.

"No," Longarm said. "I've been there several times, but my companion has never seen it before."

The man appeared to be in his late twenties, dressed in a well-tailored black suit and wearing a fashionable black derby. He smiled at Milly. "It is rare that I get a chance to ride with such lovely company. My name is Brian Ballard. And I would imagine you and this gentleman are married."

"Then you'd imagine wrong," Milly said. "But that might be in store for our futures. I am pleased to make your acquaintance, Mr. Ballard, I am Miss Milly Ott and this is Marshal Custis Long. We are from Denver."

"Well, what is a *marshal* from Colorado doing all the way out here in Nevada?"

"Actually I'm *not* here in an official capacity."

"Odd time of the year to visit the Comstock Lode, given this foul weather."

"Sometimes," Longarm replied, not liking to answer personal questions posed by a stranger, "you have to go see places when your schedule permits. And what, sir, is *your* reason for visiting Virginia City?"

"I recently inherited quite a few shares of a mine that was once quite profitable. It's called the Sentinel Mine and it's been closed for several years, after there was a cave-in and some flooding on the lower levels. I've come to see if the mine can be reopened profitably and if its shares are still worth anything close to their former value. If the answers to those questions are positive, I'll report to some of my friends and fellow investors, and we might reopen the Sentinel."

"As you very well know," Longarm said, "most of the big pockets of ore below Sun Mountain have been picked clean."

"Of course, but there is something about a gold mine that fires the imagination and enthusiasm."

"It's called gold fever," Longarm said, noting the man's gold jewelry. "And it's been around probably as long as mankind."

"I'm sure that's true. Stocks rise and fall, but gold has a lasting value anywhere in the world."

"Well," Milly said, "I certainly hope that you find the Sentinel to still be of value. Do you know anything about deep rock mining?"

"Not much," Ballard admitted. "But I've learned to rely on local experts. I'm sure that I'll soon be directed toward people whose opinion on gold mining can be taken seriously."

Longarm smiled but thought that if he had ever seen a man with money who was ripe for the plucking, Brian Ballard was it.

"Mr. Ballard," Milly asked, "have you come from a great distance?"

"I'm from Seattle. My father and I own an import business, but he recently had a serious stroke and, sadly, is no longer able to make crucial business decisions."

"What kind of things do you import?"

"Asian jewelry. Jade, silver, and gold."

"I noticed that ring you are wearing," Milly said, pointing at Brian Ballard's hand. "It's really beautiful."

"Thank you." Ballard extended his hand so that she could better see the large jade stone, surrounded by diamonds and gold. "This ring has always been one of my favorites, and it dates back to the Ming Dynasty, which makes it very old and quite rare."

Milly's eyes grew wide with wonder. "I've never seen anything like it! Have you, Custis?"

"Can't say that I have. Mr. Ballard, may I offer you a piece of professional advice?"

"Please call me Brian. And yes, I welcome all well-intended and sound advice."

"I'd hide the ring. Same for that gold watch and chain that looks like they cost a small fortune."

"Mind telling me why?"

"Virginia City and the Comstock are undergoing hard times, and there are going to be many pickpockets and thugs in town desperate to find a well-heeled mark."

Brian Ballard nodded, his expression grave. "I see."

"Of course," Longarm added, "I could be mistaken,

but I am certain that you would be quickly targeted by thieves, or worse, before you've gotten off this stage-coach and walked a block."

To Ballard's credit, he removed his ring and pocket watch and dropped them into his pocket. "I appreciate the advice. Any chance that you would . . . um, accompany me for the few days that I'll be on the Comstock? I'd pay you very well."

"Sorry," Longarm told the man. "But we have some things that we have come a long way to take care of and they're likely to keep us busy."

"I understand. Are you and Miss Ott going to be staying on the Comstock Lode for very long?"

"Only," Longarm told the man, "as long as is necessary and then we will be returning to Denver."

Ballard looked out the window at the sage and the few remaining stunted piñon and juniper. "I have to say that I'm rather shocked at how desolate this country is in comparison to where I come from. My first impression is that I would rather sell the Sentinel Mine if it has any value and then leave."

"It's a hard place to make a living," Longarm said. "But men have been doing it for quite a while up here. In its heyday, the Comstock Lode made a dozen or more men millionaires."

"So I've heard. Have either of you ever been to Seattle?"

"No," Milly said. "But I hear it is beautiful."

"That it is." Ballard looked out the window as the stage began to roll. "I'm not used to this really cold weather. In Seattle it almost never snows."

"No," Longarm commented, "but it's foggy with a climate that chills right to the marrow of the bone."

Ballard shrugged, clearly not in agreement. "I think we're all partial to our own environments. The Silver Dollar Hotel and Saloon was recommended to me by someone who had been here several years ago. Perhaps you'll end up staying there as well and we could have dinner together . . . my treat . . . of course."

"That would be very nice," Milly said quickly. "Wouldn't that be splendid, Custis?"

"Sure," he replied without enthusiasm because, in Longarm's experience, it was better if he did not encourage friendships when he was working. The less people knew about his business the better.

"Good!" Ballard said, as they began to roll by mine tailings and abandoned mining operations, shacks, and rusty and abandoned old mining equipment.

Longarm turned his attention to the passing scenery as Milly and Brian Ballard chatted about this and that. Ballard was, Longarm decided, honest and telling the truth about his Seattle import business. Ballard enthralled Milly with stories about his past travels, to Japan and China and other exotic places in Asia.

When they rolled up Virginia City's famous C Street, Longarm saw that a few of the town's former businesses had been closed and shuttered. Still, the street was jammed with heavy ore wagons heading for the stamping mills, and right in the center of the town, all the big saloons that he remembered were open and looked to be busy. The coach stopped near the V&T Railroad depot, and they disembarked.

Brian Ballard was handed his baggage and stood looking as if he were trying to make a big decision.

"Something wrong?" Longarm asked.

"No, it's just that we passed Silver Dollar Hotel, and I have to say that it wasn't at all what I had expected."

"A saloon and a hotel are usually a bad match," Longarm said. "The upstairs rooms are primarily used for the girls to service customers. I think you might want to consider tagging along with us to the Oxford Hotel. I've stayed there in the past and it's clean and safe. They don't have a restaurant, but there are several nearby."

Ballard looked all around and noted several men loitering and drinking in the vicinity. He was not a big man, and Longarm would have bet he had never worked one hard day in his entire life. And even though he had taken Longarm's advice and removed his expensive jewelry, it was still obvious from his clothing and handsome luggage that he was a man of means.

"I . . . I would be happy to go along with you," Ballard said, nodding with gratitude.

"Good then," Longarm said. "Let's set off up the hill and find that hotel. I don't know about you two, but it's dinnertime and I'm ready for a drink and something good to eat."

"Remember," Ballard said, "tonight is on me."

"Oh, we'll remember," Milly said with a laugh. "Don't worry about that."

Three rough-looking men who had been lounging near the depot suddenly cut them off at the bottom of the short hill they had to climb.

"Excuse me," one of the men said, eyeing Milly up

and down and then turning to Brian Ballard. "Me and my friends here have had a little hard luck lately, and we were wondering if you nice gentlemen could spare us a few dollars. We'd pay you back, of course."

Ballard managed a thin smile and started to reach for his wallet, but Longarm stepped in front of the man. "We're tired and in a hurry. Step aside."

The man was big enough and tough enough to bluster. "Well, I think that you are completely lacking in manners, sir. And besides, I was particularly addressing this other gentleman."

"Move aside," Longarm ordered in a hard voice.

The man glanced at his two companions, and something seemed to pass between them, because all three armed themselves with knives in addition to brass knuckles.

"Now," the man said, "I think you had better be the one to move aside."

Longarm's left fist shot out like the head of a snake and his knuckles smashed into the man's nose, breaking it and sending the man reeling backward. When the other two jumped forward, Longarm's right hand crossed his belt buckle and snapped his Colt from its holster on his left hip. The gun came up and the two men dropped their knives in the dirt and fled.

The man whose nose Longarm had smashed in was cupping it with both hands, blood dripping between his fingers.

"Damn you!" the injured man cried. "We only wanted a couple of lousy dollars!"

"Tell you what," Longarm said, "I'll give you something that will last longer than a few dollars."

"What . . ."

Longarm smashed the barrel of his heavy Colt across the man's forehead, knocking him out cold.

"My god!" Brian Ballard whispered. "Don't you think that you might have hurt him badly?"

"Oh, I did that all right," Longarm agreed as he watched the other pair stop and turn to see if they were going to be shot or chased. "But the thing is, Brian, you have to kind of set up the ground rules when you come to a boom town as rough as this one. Even as we speak, the news of what I did to this one will have begun being passed up and down all the streets, and guess what?"

"What?"

"We won't be bothered anymore," Longarm said, holstering his pistol and starting up the hill into town.

"Custis!" Milly said, hurrying to catch up with him. "That man will need stitches in his scalp, and his nose is really a mess!"

"You think I was too rough on him, do you?"

Milly glanced back over her shoulder at the man, who was kneeling in the dirt, sobbing and holding his ruined face. "Well . . . well I just think that you didn't need to beat him with your pistol *in addition* to breaking his nose."

Longarm didn't even break stride to answer. "Milly, I told you that you wouldn't be prepared for what faced us up here. We haven't even come face-to-face with the worst of it yet and already you're starting to tell me what to do and what not to do."

"I don't mean to do that, Custis, but you really hurt that man!"

"And what do you think they intended to do with those knives they pulled? Clip our fingernails?"

Milly didn't have a reply, and as Longarm hiked up the hill with the woman and the gentleman from Seattle struggling along behind, he was sure wishing that he had not been seduced into dragging along Milly Ott and perhaps now another person he was going to have to worry about protecting.

Chapter 20

It was early when Longarm awoke the next morning, and Milly was still asleep, so he quietly dressed and left the hotel. Virginia City and Gold Hill were separated by the Summit, which was actually the crest of a hill. Freight coming from Carson City had to make the long pull up the canyon and over the Summit to enter Virginia City. Freight coming from Reno to Gold Hill had to descend the steep quarter-mile descent, and many an accident had occurred where conditions were especially treacherous during snowy and icy winters.

Longarm had a good heavy coat and woolen gloves, and he'd bought some boots that would offer him excellent footing. Even so, in the cold not long after dawn, each step he took toward the Summit was a challenge. He knew the temperature was still well below the freezing point.

"Hey!"

Longarm turned around, collar up and hat tugged down low. He saw a man driving a pair of horses pulling a buckboard. The man came to a stop next to him. "Need a ride down to Carson City?"

Longarm looked up to see a scarf covering the lower half of the man's face and a wool stocking cap covering the top half. Only the driver's eyes and nose were visible. "I'm only going down to Gold Hill, but I'd appreciate a ride even that far."

"Hop aboard! Once over the Summit the road is steep and pretty damned icy; you'd be sure to take a few falls before you got down into Gold Canyon."

"Much obliged," Longarm said, climbing up onto the seat and noting that the buckboard was filled with lumber. "How are you going to keep this buckboard from going into a slide and running over your team?"

"Ain't easy, but I do it once a day all winter. Got a good pair of brakes and the horses have ice shoes with little spikes for grabbers. Don't worry, mister, we won't go sledding down the hill out of control."

"Nice to hear you say that," Longarm said.

"If you don't mind my askin', what kind of business in Gold Hill brings you out at such an early hour?"

"I'm looking for a couple of men."

"Friends?"

"Not exactly. They're brothers and mule skinners."

"I know a pair of men that *look* like brothers and are mule skinners. Probably ain't the same ones you're lookin' for."

"Might be they changed their names," Longarm offered. "What do they look like?"

"They're big, dark, and ugly. I had one almost drive

me over the side of this road a week or so ago. I was pulling toward the top of the Summit, and he came roarin' over the crest with four mules and a heavy load of ore. His mules were havin' a hell of a time and the ore wagon was slidin' all over the road. I shouted at the man and told him to slow down and show some good sense."

"What did he do?"

"He said something to me that is not worth repeating. But everyone knows that Dirk is an asshole."

Longarm felt a jolt of excitement shoot through his half-frozen body. "That would be Dirk Pierce?"

"Yeah. You know him?"

"I know of him. And is the one that looks like him named Harold York?"

"We call him Harry. It's a fitting name because he's as hairy as a gorilla. Not that I'm ever goin' to see a real gorilla, but I seen pictures of them and he's that hairy."

"I need to find them."

The buckboard driver didn't speak for several minutes as he carefully drove his horses down the steepest part of the winding road toward Gold Hill. Finally, when the grade flattenedd a bit, he said, "They worked for the Catamount Mining Company."

" 'Worked'?"

"Yeah. They got fired a few days ago."

"Any idea where they might have gone?" Longarm asked, feeling the excitement die.

"As a matter of fact I do. Dirk and Harry got hired on by the V and T Railroad down in Carson City. They are hauling timber out of the Sierra foothills south of town. Railroad needs timber to make railroad ties and build bridges. They pay pretty good; the work is hard but steady, and I've been thinking of trying to get on with them."

"Well," Longarm said, "I guess that I will be going all the way to Carson City with you."

"Nice to have the company on such a cold, dreary day," the man said. "My name is Wade Talbert."

"Custis Long."

"I take it you're not a freighter," Talbert said.

"What makes you think I'm not?"

"Well, you asked me right away if we were going to slide off the road up near the Summit. A driver would know that anyone pulling up or down that grade would have to have his horses shoed with cleats and ice spikes."

"I guess a driver would."

They were passing through Gold Hill, which looked about half the size that it had the last time Longarm had visited. Still, there were three saloons, and every one of them was open even at this early hour in the morning. The Red Ass Café was open, and through its dirty front window Longarm saw that it was doing a good breakfast business. Two men bundled up against the cold were standing outside the door waiting for a table, and when they saw Talbert, they waved and called out a greeting.

Talbert waved back but didn't slow.

"Are there many mines still producing in Gold Hill and Virginia City?"

"A few," Talbert answered. "Mostly just the deepest

ones with the most money to keep digging. Last I heard the Ophir was down to eight hundred and fifty feet."

"That's mighty deep," Longarm said. "I imagine it's hotter than hell down that far."

"It is," Talbert agreed. "The Comstock Lode Miner's Union has it in their contract that every miner on every shift working deeper than five hundred feet gets to be given a big bucket of ice or snow. But at temperatures well over a hundred and ten degrees, they say that the ice and snow is gone in twenty or thirty minutes."

"I don't know how men can stand working down there at those temperatures."

"They're desperate people and they need jobs. Me, I've always been a freighter and I'll die one. It's a job that you can do right up to the end unless the company you work for expects you to load and unload your own wagon." "Yours doesn't?"

"Nope. I told them that they'd better not expect it, either. I've had too many friends who caved in to loading and unloading every wagon they drove, and they all ended up with real bad backs that wouldn't take the jolting of a wagon. They either have to find some lesser job or they'll starve. But not me."

Longarm and Wade Talbert carried on a pleasant conversation all the way off Sun Mountain and down into the high desert. By noon, they were pulling into Carson City.

"You been here before?" Talbert asked.

"Yeah, but not for a few years."

"It hasn't changed much," the driver said. "Carson City is still a real nice town. My wife and I live back up in Gold Hill, but the water tastes terrible and the ground is so rocky you can't raise so much as a tomato all summer. Too much alkali in the water and earth. That water will make you sick if you drink more than a few cups of it. We have all our drinking water brought up from Carson City. The water down here is good and comes from wells dug along the Carson River. My wife can't wait to move down here, soon as I get another job."

"Where is the V and T Railroad headquarters?"

"Right over there." Talbert pointed to a big stone building near a roundhouse. "Want me to drive you right up to their door?"

"Not necessary," Longarm told the friendly driver. "It's warmed up enough that the ice is melting and I'll be just fine walking."

"Well, hope you don't get into too much trouble," the driver said. "Dirk and Harry have bad reputations, and I hear that they're mean and deadly fighters. That's why I didn't get off this wagon when Dirk started cussin' me out at the Summit, even though he was clearly in the wrong. No sense in gettin' your ass carved up or stomped in the snow over nothin' that important, is there?"

"Nope," Longarm said, "no sense at all."

"I ain't afraid of any man, but I got a wife to take care of and we're expecting our first child this spring. That's why I let that man cuss me out so bad."

"You did the right thing, Talbert. A man has to walk away from a fight sometimes when others depend on his health for their livelihood."

"Well I'm glad to hear you say that 'cause I've been

chafin' some at lettin' another man insult me and do at me so bad."

"Maybe I can set things right for you," Longarm said. "I'm all alone and don't have a wife and a baby coming to worry about."

"Well, don't do nothin' stupid on my account," Talbert offered. "I feel bad enough about backin' down, and I'd feel even worse if I thought what I told you got you killed or hurt real bad."

"I'll be fine."

"I hope so. Just . . . just be careful if you try to collect money from either of 'em or have a bone to pick," Talbert warned. "You're big and strong . . . but so are they."

"Thanks for the warning."

Longarm climbed down from the buckboard and headed toward the railroad's headquarters. He unbuttoned the buttons on his overcoat and removed his gloves, folded them, and stuffed them into his coat pocket. If he suddenly came upon the Raney brothers, he would draw his weapon and arrest them on the spot. If they resisted and wanted a fight, he'd not hesitate to put them in the ground six feet under the ice, mud, and snow.

If he did that, Wade Talbert sure wouldn't have to worry about them if he got a better job hauling timbers for the V&T Railroad.

Chapter 21

"So you're lookin' for Dirk Pierce and Harold York, huh?" the older man in the V&T Railroad headquarters said suspiciously.

"That's right."

"What for?"

Longarm had realized many years ago that there were some people that you liked at first sight and others that irritated you the moment you met them. This pompous little man fit in the latter category. But nevertheless he ground his teeth and managed to say, "I've got some past business to settle with them."

The man was short and bald, with little wire-rimmed spectacles and a little red bobbin for a nose. "Look," he said, sizing Longarm up. "If you're the law, then I want you to know right off that we don't have anything to do with their behavior outside this job. We don't ask 'em much about their past, and we don't promise them any rose garden for their future.

All that we care about here is if they are honest, hard-working, and can do the job that we hire 'em for."

"Is that it?" Longarm managed to ask.

"Is *what* it?"

"The speech you just gave. I was wondering if I had to listen to any more of your company-line bullshit."

The V&T man flushed with anger. "I don't much care for your attitude, mister. You come in here and take up my valuable time and then you get smart-assed with me."

Longarm reached out with both hands and grabbed the man's prominent ears. He twisted them hard enough that the man squealed in pain, and when he tried to pull back, Longarm yanked his face up close.

"Listen, you self-important little turd. I'm the law all right, and I've tracked those two men all the way from Denver. Their names aren't Pierce and York; they are brothers named Dirk and Harold Raney. But the most important thing you need to know is that if you don't answer my questions, I'm going to twist your big ears around so that you'll *permanently* only hear from behind."

"Ouch! Oh, gawd! Let me go! Please! Help!"

There were other men in the office, but Longarm had acted so quickly they were all stunned and frozen with indecision.

"Answer my question!" Longarm hissed.

"They're on the job hauling timber out of the foot-hills!" the man cried. "They make one trip a day!"

"When are they due back?"

"By four or five o'clock!"

Longarm released the man and planted his hands

on the counter. "I'll wait for them right here," he decided. "You have any problem with that?"

"Gosh no, not me!"

"Good. I'll take that seat over there by the potbellied stove. A cup of coffee would be appreciated."

The man rubbed his red ears and in a petulant voice asked, "Are you a Pinkerton man or a federal marshal, and what did they do?"

"They killed a woman and a policeman in Baltimore," Longarm said. "And I'm damn sure they killed a man in Rawlins and probably a lot more that I don't know about."

"Oh my gawd!"

"Coffee," Longarm growled. "Black and strong."

"Yes, sir!"

Longarm took a chair and accepted a cup of coffee, which was good and hot. He wondered what was going on up in Virginia City with Milly Ott and faulted himself for not at least leaving her a note. She was a good woman, and the idea of accepting Mayor Plummer's five thousand dollars reward money and hooking up with the woman on a permanent basis was starting to nibble at his mind. A man could do a lot worse than to change his life by marrying such a pretty and loving woman and getting a ten-thousand-dollar start to boot.

Yep, a man could do a whole hell of a lot worse, Longarm thought as he sipped coffee and reached for a newspaper that was folded close at hand.

Milly Ott wasn't prepared to wake up alone. She had slept very late, and now she hurried to get dressed and go downstairs, where she expected Custis would be waiting for her. Today would be a very important day . . . probably the most important in her entire life.

Today they would find and kill the Raney brothers and then send a telegraph to Mayor Plummer in Denver apprising him of that fact and asking that their respective five thousand dollars in reward money be sent by telegram to either Reno, Virginia City, or perhaps Carson City. Mayor Plummer would no doubt insist on proof of the deaths of the Raney brothers, but Milly had already figured that one out.

They would get a local judge to certify that the Raney brothers were indeed dead. If necessary, they would find the local mayor and any other officials that Mayor Plummer might require before he was satisfied that his long quest for restitution had been satisfied.

"Milly!"

She was in the hotel lobby and turned to see Brian Ballard coming to meet her. "Good morning," he said.

"I'm afraid that I've really overslept this morning," she told him. "Have you seen Custis around?"

"No, but someone else saw him leave very early this morning."

"To go to breakfast?"

"No," Brian said, "he was last seen boarding a buckboard headed over the Summit."

"Oh my gawd! He went after the Raney brothers all on his own!"

Brian Ballard saw her look of shock and consternation. "What's wrong? Is there something that I can help you with?"

Milly took a deep breath. "I need coffee and something to eat," she said. "Brian, what I'm about to tell you is going to be confidential and important. Can you keep a secret?"

"Of course."

"Then let's go find some breakfast . . . or I suppose lunch is more to the hour . . . and I'll tell you everything."

"I'm at your service," he said, taking her arm.

Thirty minutes later they were seated in a Virginia City café, and Milly told her new young friend from Seattle all about the Raney brothers and about Mayor Plummer and his badly wounded son back in Denver.

"I made Marshal Long . . . who by the way gave up his badge but admits that he is still a federal marshal with that authority . . . bring me here to find and help him either kill or arrest the Raney brothers."

"But you just said that the mayor wants them *dead*."

"Yes, because I doubt that if we brought them back to Denver for a trial, they'd be convicted and sentenced to hang. You see, we don't have evidence that they murdered that man in Rawlins, and we don't have anyone other than Henry Plummer to even identify them as the murderers of his mother and that policeman so long ago. And that is why the mayor really wants them tracked down and *shot*."

"What a story. And you think that Custis Long has gone after them this morning?"

"I'm sure of it. The Raney brothers were supposed to be working for a freighting company in Gold Hill. That must be where Custis went to find and I hope to kill them."

"Then we should go there."

"Yes," Milly said, finishing her breakfast, "we should at once. Would you mind hiring someone to deliver us down to Gold Hill?"

Brian Ballard nodded, but his expression was troubled. Noticing it, Milly said, "I see that I've badly upset you with my confession. I'm sorry. You've come all the way from Seattle to the Comstock Lode to evaluate your mine's potential for profit, and I'm here to try to see that two murderers are caught and killed."

Brian Ballard swallowed hard and stared down at his napkin for a moment. "Milly, now that you've been so totally honest with me, I have a confession of my own to make."

"I . . ."

He took a deep breath. "The truth of it is that I don't even have the money to hire us a conveyance down to Gold Hill."

"What!"

"I'm almost dead broke," he said quietly.

"But what about the Asian import business and your investor friends and . . ."

"I do have a little import business in Seattle, but it barely affords me a living. And the reason I've scrimped and saved up for the last few years and bought all the expensive clothes that I'm wearing is that I did inherit some mining stock and I was desperately hoping . . . gambling really . . . that it was still worth several thousand dollars."

"Well, isn't it?"

"No," he said. "Last night I went to a saloon and asked about the Sentinel Mine, and I was told that it was abandoned years ago and all of its equipment was sold to debtors for pennies on the dollar. The mine is just an open pit now, used by the city as a dump for refuse. The Sentinel Mine is closed and will never be reopened."

Milly groaned. "So your stock is . . ."

"Not worth the paper it's printed upon," Brian said sadly. "In fact, I was told that there are still creditors hoping to recoup some of their investments and that I would be wise to leave Virginia City before they caught wind that I was here in town."

"So you're *penniless*?"

"Nearly. I have about six dollars, and I was wise enough to have bought a round-trip ticket back to Seattle. But other than that and my small business and a little cottage that I did inherit, I've nothing."

"Oh, damn," Milly uttered. "I'm really sorry to hear that."

"I'll survive, and in fact I expect that if I work hard and long enough, my little import business will dramatically expand. I didn't dare hinge all my hopes for prosperity on the Sentinel Mine. And I'm not one to go into a bottle with this Comstock Lode setback. I guess I was just hoping to get rich quick."

Milly reached into her purse. "I'm buying our breakfast."

"I have enough to do that," he argued.

"No, you spent a lot of money that you couldn't afford on Custis and me last night, and I am going to buy your breakfast."

"Last night at dinner, I was filled with optimism and certain that the Sentinel Mine was still valuable. What foolish optimism."

"Never you mind that," Milly said, laying her hand on his. "You're a fine man, and it's clear to me that you are a gentleman who will go far in this world."

He looked up with hope in his blue eyes. "Do you *really* think so?"

"I'd bet on it," Milly said, leaving enough money on the table. "Now, I understand that Gold Hill is less than a half mile from where we are sitting. I don't know about you, but I'm stuffed and could use a good, brisk walk."

"So could I."

"Then let's walk over the Summit to Gold Hill and just hope and pray that Custis Long has found and shot those Raney brothers dead, so that he and I can each collect a five-thousand-dollar reward."

"That sounds like a fine idea," Brian Ballard said, rising and offering Milly his arm.

Such a gentleman and, although not big or nearly as strong as Custis, really quite handsome, Milly thought as they set out to find Gold Hill and Custis Long.

Chapter 22

"Oh, dear gawd!" cried the V&T officer whose ears Longarm had twisted so hard. "Here they come!" He whirled around and shouted to the others in the office. "Everyone get down on the floor and stay down!"

Longarm thought that advice was probably sound as he slipped his gun out of his holster, checked it one more time, and then finished his coffee. Speaking to no one in particular, he said, "I'm going to arrest them outside so that it will be safer. Still, if the bullets start to fly, a stray could come through the front window. So everyone should stay down."

"Can't you just arrest them?" the man whined. "I mean, isn't that what a lawman or a Pinkerton agent is *supposed* to do?"

"It never quite works out like you expect," Longarm said, pushing back his coat and stepping outside to close the door behind him.

The Raney brothers were big and bundled up in

heavy, muddy buffalo robes. They were each driving
a logging wagon pulled by eight mud-spattered mules.
Their loads of thick pine logs had all been trimmed
but not yet peeled of their bark.

Longarm wasn't a man to hesitate and look for the
perfect moment to go into action. He slogged across
the snowy yard and stopped thirty feet in front of the
two approaching wagons.

"Hold up there!"

"Move aside, you asshole!" one of the brothers
yelled. "Or by gawd I'll run you over!"

Longarm drew his Colt and pointed it at the nearer
man. "I'm a United States federal marshal and you are
the Raney brothers wanted for murder. Pull in your
teams, set your brakes, and raise your hands!"

The brothers didn't do *anything* that Longarm
demanded. Instead of pulling in their mule teams, they
whipped them forward. Even though each was pulling
a heavy load through snow, ice, and mud, both mule
teams lurched forward with surprising speed. Longarm fired, pivoted to move out of the way, and slipped
in the slush. He fell heavily and looked up to see the
mules coming straight at him.

He rolled out of their path and the teams charged
past on both sides. The Raney brothers were armed
and tried to fire downward into his body.

But their wild shots off a moving wagon were bad
misses. Longarm saw the brothers bail out of their
wagons, hit the snow, and roll. Both men began firing,
but so did Longarm.

The footing was unstable, and Longarm was covered with slush and mud. He had loaded all six cylin-

ders and now used three shots on each man, alternating between them and watching them jerk, stumble, and twist with every bullet's impact. When his gun was empty, Longarm dropped to one knee and pulled out his two-shot derringer. One of the brothers was still on his feet, still coming forward, and Longarm fired both barrels of his deadly little gun.

The last brother took Longarm's final bullet squarely in the face and pitched over backward into the snow.

It was over.

Shaking with the cold and wet, Longarm slogged up to the corpses and searched them for more weapons and valuables. He found Bowie knives and pistols, which he tossed on top of the freshly cut stacks of logs.

Slowly, employees began to emerge from the V&T Railroad headquarters. They began to whisper and cautiously approached the humped and shaggy bodies that reminded Longarm of freshly slain buffalo.

"What are you going to do now?" the little man with the red ears finally dared to asked.

Longarm pulled on his gloves and carefully wiped mud and snow from his coat. He considered the question for a moment. "You got any more of that hot coffee?"

"Yes, sir!"

"I'm cold and I'd like another cup," he said to no one in particular as he turned and walked slowly back to the office.

The telegram from Denver came within hours of the one that Longarm and Milly Ott sent to the mayor's office. The next day several more were exchanged, not only between the immediate parties but between Nevada's territorial governor and Carson City's town marshal. And finally, ten thousand dollars was wired directly from Mayor Plummer's personal bank account to Longarm and Milly Ott, along with this surprising news:

> THANK YOU FOR GIVING ME AND MY SON
> RETRIBUTION **STOP** MY SON HENRY IS FAST
> RECOVERING FROM HIS GUNSHOTS **STOP** HIS
> MARRIAGE PROPOSAL TO MRS. DELIA FLANNERY
> ACCEPTED **STOP** YOU ARE BOTH INVITED TO THE
> JUNE WEDDING **STOP** ENJOY YOUR WELL-EARNED
> MONETARY REWARDS

Longarm was smiling broadly when he showed the telegram and handed over a five-thousand-dollar check to Milly Ott. "Can you believe that?" he asked with amazement. "Henry Plummer proposed to Delia Flannery and we're invited to their June wedding. Won't that be something?"

Milly looked away for a moment before turning back to him and saying, "I'm afraid I won't be able to attend the wedding."

"Why not?"

Now she lifted her chin and met his eyes. "Brian has asked me to become his wife and go back to Seattle. We're going to invest my five thousand in his business and buy a nice big house."

Longarm's jaw dropped. "Are you serious?"

"Never been more serious. I'm sorry, Custis. But

after thinking over all you've said and done since we've been together, I realized that you're never going to become happily settled into marriage and a family."

"With ten thousand dollars, I was giving that some serious consideration."

"Go back to Denver and do good with your share of the reward," she said, then added, "and Brian and I wouldn't mind if you used a little of that reward money to give us a nice Seattle wedding present."

Longarm folded his check and put it in his pocket. "Count on it, Milly. And give my congratulations to Brian. I don't know him, but my first impression was all good."

"And now what will you do?"

"I'm going home," he said. "I've got a room, a cat, and a nice, loving woman waiting."

"Then buy her something grand and put the rest of that reward money in your savings account. You know that you can't always be a United States deputy marshal."

"No," he said, "I don't know."

And with that, Longarm headed back to his hotel to get his bags. Carson City was a nice town, but for his money, Denver was where he really belonged, and he was missing Irene.

Watch for

LONGARM AND THE
DEADWOOD SHOOT-OUT

the 411th novel in the exciting LONGARM
series from Jove
Coming in February!

And Don't Miss

LONGARM AND THE
AMBUSH AT HOLY DEFIANCE

Longarm GIANT Edition 2013
Available from Jove in February!

GIANT-SIZED ADVENTURE FROM
AVENGING ANGEL LONGARM.

BY TABOR EVANS

2006 Giant Edition:

LONGARM AND THE
OUTLAW EMPRESS

2007 Giant Edition:

LONGARM AND
THE GOLDEN EAGLE
SHOOT-OUT

2008 Giant Edition:

LONGARM AND THE
VALLEY OF SKULLS

2009 Giant Edition:

LONGARM AND THE
LONE STAR TRACKDOWN

2010 Giant Edition:

LONGARM AND THE
RAILROAD WAR

2013 Giant Edition:

LONGARM AND
THE AMBUSH AT HOLY
DEFIANCE

penguin.com/actionwesterns

M456AS0812

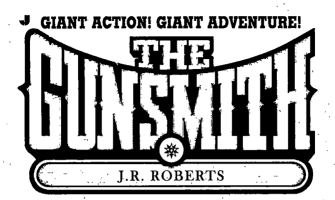

GIANT ACTION! GIANT ADVENTURE!

THE GUNSMITH

J.R. ROBERTS

DON'T MISS A YEAR OF

Slocum Giant
by
Jake Logan

penguin.com/actionwesterns

M457AS0812

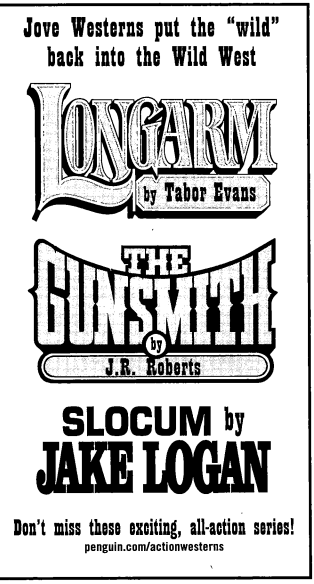